Confounding Caroline

Confounding Caroline

A Pride and Prejudice Variation

LEENIE BROWN

LEENIE B BOOKS

HALIFAX

Contents

Dear Reader,

Once upon a time...well, actually, a couple of years ago, I began a weekly writing exercise on my blog (leeniebrown.com) and called it Thursday's Three Hundred. What was supposed to be just a few minutes of practice – just three hundred words a week – quickly took on a life of its own and became something much grander.

To date, those writing exercises have produced one short story (*Hope at Dawn*), a four-book series (*Willow Hall Romance*), a stand-alone novella (*With the Colonel's Help*) and now, this novella that you hold in your hand, which is either the first of a pair of stories or the beginning of something a bit longer.

While some things about how I create these stories have evolved since that first writing exercise, the tradition of posting a portion of a work in progress continues each Thursday. In fact, there is a new story posting there now.

Chapter 1

Fitzwilliam Darcy handed his coat and beaver to his friend's butler, while that friend, Charles Bingley, leaned nonchalantly against the sitting room's door frame. The soft glow of a lamp, which remained lit, shone behind him, indicating that Bingley had been engaged in some activity in the room before which he now stood.

"I had hoped you would be home, but I did not expect it," Darcy said in greeting. It was not Bingley's normal wont to remain at home. "Reading?" he queried with some surprise as he took note of the book in Bingley's hand.

Bingley shrugged. "I do read on occasion."

"I would not wish to keep you from your amusements." Darcy smirked slightly. If he knew his friend, Bingley would likely not mind the disruption since Bingley preferred people to books.

Bingley shook his head and chuckled. "Come, my study would be more comfortable than the sitting room and less likely to be invaded by females should Caroline return early."

"I am surprised you did not accompany her to the Grahams' soiree," Darcy said as he followed Bingley into the study.

"I have had my fill of ferrying Caroline around only to have her turn up her pert little nose at every gentleman she meets, so I sent her with Louisa and Hurst."

He tucked his book away on a shelf behind his desk, and then opening the door on the right side of his desk, he pulled out a bottle of amber coloured liquid and two glasses.

"I find I tire of society. It is always the same. The same ladies in different dresses with different coloured hair and hats, but the same gossip, the same weather, the same pleasantries. It's just so much of the same, over and over and over and over." He handed a glass to Darcy and smiled. "Besides, if I am not mistaken, I will not be the only one who will enjoy this Caroline-free evening."

Darcy chuckled "The quiet is agreeable to me, but you have never enjoyed silence so much as I."

There was something different about Bingley the past few weeks. He did not smile as much as was his usual wont, and he seemed to tuck himself away in his study more and more. Darcy swirled the liquid in his glass and threw one leg over the other. The leather squeaked as he shifted in the chair across from Bingley.

Bingley sighed. "I find I am longing for the country, but Caroline will hear nothing of leaving town when there are so many functions to attend." He took a draught from his glass. "If I thought she meant to find a husband, trotting her around to the various venues might not be so bothersome, but she is not intent on snaring anyone but you."

Darcy knew that fact very well. Caroline had never been reserved in demonstrating her preference for him over every gentleman she met. "A title and a larger fortune might dissuade her."

The hint of bitterness in Bingley's laugh surprised Darcy almost as much as Bingley's wishing to leave town and avoid society. These were not Bingley actions. They were behaviours that were more likely to be attributed to Darcy rather than his gregarious friend.

"She is as stubborn as a mule," Bingley muttered, "and almost as bright."

Darcy's brows rose. He was not surprised by the fact that Bingley was complaining about his sister. He had heard Bingley complain about Caroline before — many times. However, he had never heard Bingley complain about anything more than her incessant need to purchase fripperies and dresses or the way she nattered on about this person or that. There was something decidedly wrong with his friend, and Darcy had a sinking feeling that he knew just what it was.

"You surprise me," Darcy said, not wishing to broach the topic of the cause of the change in Bingley but knowing it was necessary. "Was it not you who claimed to be happy wherever you were, be it town or country?"

"That was before," Bingley said over the rim of his glass.

"Before what?" Darcy prodded.

"Before I took an estate." Bingley shifted in his chair uneasily, studying the painting above the fireplace for a few moments before allowing his attention to return to his friend. He sighed deeply as his gaze fell to where Darcy's foot slowly bounced up and down.

Surreptitiously, Darcy glanced at his friend. He recognized Bingley's sigh, for it was the same groan of uncertainty that had taken up residence in his own chest. It was a new and unwelcome feeling, and it was not something that, though he had tried, he could command away. He had not been able to erase it with busyness, nor had he been able to wash it away with drink. There remained only one option for dealing with such uncertainty and its pretty reason. It must be acknowledged for what it was. The root of it must be exposed, then left to wither away with time — at least, for him. For his friend, he hoped for a different outcome.

"Is it the estate or the society in Hertfordshire that you miss, my friend?" Darcy's voice was quiet, and he fixed his eyes on the wall beyond Bingley's head. A small smile played at his mouth as he contemplated the image of smiling eyes and an impertinent grin that always came to his mind when he thought of Hertfordshire. "Netherfield seems like a fine estate, and the neighbourhood was not without its enchantments." He sipped his drink and then swirled it again, watching the liquid swirl up the sides of the glass.

"I thought you loathed the inhabitants of Hertfordshire." Bingley's voice was filled with incredulity. "Is that not why you and my sisters were so hasty in joining me in town — the people are beneath us, there is no society worth keeping, that sort of thing?

Again, Darcy's brows rose at the rancor in Bingley's voice. He sighed heavily, and colour crept up his cheeks. This would not be a pleasant discussion.

"I did not loathe all of the inhabitants. I found some of them to be quite delightful — so delightful, in fact, that leaving seemed safer than staying." He rose and walked to the window. Admitting his folly and weakness would be easier if he were able to move about and not have to face the friend whom he had, he suspected, unknowingly injured.

Bingley drummed his fingers on the arm of his chair and raised a brow in anticipation of an expected explanation.

"She is here in town." Darcy placed his empty glass on a side table and allowed his eyes to remain on it rather than look at his friend.

"Who is here in town?"

Darcy drew a deep breath and spared Bingley only a glance before returning his gaze to his glass. "Miss Bennet."

"Miss Bennet?"

Darcy nodded.

"How do you know?" Bingley was on his feet and pacing. "Have you seen her?"

Darcy shook his head and sighed. "No, I have not seen her, but your sisters have." He turned once again toward the window. Bingley's reaction to the news was as expected and proved to Darcy how deeply attached his friend was to Miss Bennet.

"My sisters?" Bingley stood beside his friend, his brows drawn together in question.

Darcy turned toward him. "This afternoon, while you were out, I came by to drop off those papers." He pointed to the packet sitting unopened on the somewhat cluttered desk. "Caroline informed me that Miss Bennet had called."

"She was here? Miss Bennet was here?" Bingley's eyes were wide with astonishment. "Why did Caroline not tell me?"

Darcy wished to walk away from his friend, so that he could not see the pain in Bingley's eyes, but he would not. "It seems your sister is actively trying to separate you and Miss Bennet. She seemed to think I would be impressed by her belittling of the inferior society of the country." He paused and drew a deliberate breath. "At one time I would have agreed with her, but I no longer do."

Bingley crossed his arms and studied his friend.

Darcy winced under the examination, but it was not more than he deserved. Unable to bear both his shame and the scrutiny of his friend any longer, he turned back to the window. "I have to make a confession, Bingley. You may wish to throw me out of your home when I am finished, and I will fully understand if you do." Darcy continued to stare out the window, but he could feel the eyes of his friend boring into him.

"I wished to separate you from Miss Bennet when we left Hertfordshire." He closed his eyes as he heard his friend's muttered oath. "I told you she seemed indifferent to you. While it is true that I did not notice any particular regard for you on her part, it is not the reason I wished to separate you from her. It is not even the connection to her family or the supposed inferior society of Meryton that led me to take the actions I did." He swallowed and drew a deep fortifying breath before continuing. "I did not wish for you to become attached to Miss Bennet, for it would place me in an awkward situation. I was being completely and utterly selfish." He turned to look at his friend. "I am sorry," he whispered.

"An awkward situation?" Bingley wore a look of displeasure Darcy had rarely seen. "You would separate me from the woman I loved because it would somehow make your life awkward?"

Darcy nodded slowly. "Yes."

"Explain yourself," Bingley demanded, "for I do not have the pleasure of understanding your meaning."

Darcy shrugged one shoulder. "I thought if we left, if you and Miss Bennet were not allowed to become attached, I could avoid the danger, but I have discovered that the danger is not confined to Hertfordshire. It has followed me here to town. It haunts me day and night." He turned back towards the window as he continued.

"I am expected to marry well, to make a match that will increase the wealth and position of my family. It is what my father and uncle have always taught me."

"You are still making no sense."

Darcy could hear the exasperation in his friend's voice. It was rather how he had felt since leaving Hertfordshire — annoyed, disturbed, and vexed by the memory of Miss Elizabeth Bennet.

"How would my being fortunate enough to marry a lady such as Miss Bennet," Bingley continued, "impose upon some imagined need of yours to marry a lady of wealth and standing?"

"Miss Bennet has sisters," Darcy said to the darkness of the night before him.

"Yes, four," Bingley retorted. "I still do not see —"

"But only one," Darcy interrupted, "with the musical laughter of a brook, eyes as expressive as any the masters have painted, and a mind that is..." he shook his head "so quick, so very quick and keen."

Darcy blew out a breath. "I imagined one day I would find a woman who would meet all the qualifications my uncle and father had taught me are necessary for the wife of a man of my standing and that we would eventually learn to esteem one another. But, I cannot fathom such a match after..." His voice trailed off.

A hand grasped his shoulder. "After meeting the one person you find you do not wish to live without." It was not a question that Bingley asked but rather a statement of deep understanding.

Darcy gave his friend a sad smile and nodded mutely.

"Now, you know why I am longing for the country," Bingley said softly.

Darcy nodded again. "I suspected as much. It is why I came here tonight — to discover if I was correct. I will not stand in your way. You deserve happiness. You have been a good friend to me, and I would not want to part for any other reason." Darcy turned to leave.

"What do you mean part?" Bingley asked. "I do not hate you for what you have done if that is what has you worried. I am not happy, but I am not angry. There is no reason for us to part."

Darcy stood with his hand on the doorknob. "I do not think I can bear hearing of her, especially when she belongs to another. It is just too much." His shoulders slumped. "You shall always remain my friend, Bingley. I will always be ready to serve you in any way, but please...please, do not ask me to be a witness to that."

Chapter 2

Bingley crossed the room quickly and, taking Darcy by the shoulders, led him back to his chair. "Sit."

Darcy sighed and did as instructed.

"There is no reason for us to part," Bingley reiterated as he handed Darcy a refreshed glass of brandy.

"But —"

"No," Bingley cut Darcy off. "Duty be hanged." He dropped into his chair. There was absolutely no way while the sun still shone that he was going to lay aside his own chance at happiness with Miss Bennet, but it was equally unlikely that he was going to let a man, who was more brother than friend, walk out of his life. How would he be able to be completely happy if he knew he was the cause of such pain to Darcy?

"Your family —"

"No," Bingley cut in again. "My family, just like yours, expects me to marry well, and I shall." He smirked. "It shall, perhaps, not be as well as a certain member of my family would wish, but it is I who has to live with my choice of bride, not her. At least, I hope Caroline does not always live with me." He shuddered. She would be the next problem he would have to sort out.

"My family expects..." Darcy attempted to speak once again, only to find Bingley talking over him once more.

"I know what your family expects."

He had heard his friend wax eloquent on it many times — usually when explaining why he could not consider this or that lady whom Bingley had suggested. They were all excellent ladies. Very pleasant. Not at all stuffy and overbearing. But, none had interested Darcy in the least. Indeed, even some of the stuffier well-positioned ladies Bingley had mentioned in passing had never gotten more than a sigh and a reluctant agreement to consider them if it became necessary.

Bingley's brows drew together, and a small smile played at his lips. None of them had ever flustered

Darcy as much as Miss Elizabeth had. She had drawn him out, caused him to debate, and had even enticed him to dance. And now she was the one woman whom Darcy would regret all his life if he did not pursue and win her.

With a most serious look on his face, Bingley sat forward in his chair, leaning toward his friend. "What would happen if you did not fulfill your family's expectations? Would you be cut off? Disinherited? Shunned by society? What would the consequences be?"

Darcy shrugged and sipped his drink. "I suppose it would cause a family rift."

"Meaning you would have fewer functions to attend because they would not invite you?"

Darcy nodded. "Yes, there is that."

"Who would refuse to see you?"

Darcy drew a deep breath. "I cannot say with any certainty who would do so besides Aunt Catherine."

"But," Bingley persisted. "She will be displeased no matter whom you marry unless it is her daughter. You have said so yourself. Do you intend to marry your cousin?"

"No, I have no desire to marry Anne."

"Then marrying Miss Elizabeth would be no different from your marrying some duke's daughter." Bingley cocked his head to the side and settled back into his chair.

"It might make it more challenging for Georgiana when she comes out if my connections are not of the first circles," Darcy argued.

Bingley shrugged. "Will she not still have her thirty thousand?"

"Of course, she will."

"Will your family's ties to the land and aristocracy not still be of long standing?"

Darcy shook his head. "That is a foolish question. How would my heritage change?"

Bingley smiled. "I do not know, but you seem to think that marrying a gentleman's daughter will somehow change how a prospective husband will view Georgiana." He shrugged, rose from his chair, and paced to the window before presenting his next argument. "Actually, I am rather surprised that you would even consider a gentleman who offered for your sister only because she would be a feather in his societal cap."

Darcy's head pulled back, and he blinked.

Bingley smiled. The comment had done its

work. It had startled his friend and would hopefully get him to begin to see duty for what it was
— a weight that could drag a person down into
wretchedness. Perhaps Darcy would consider such
a fate for himself, but he would never do so for his
sister.

"You must consider her happiness," Bingley
continued, leaning against the bookshelf that was
near the window. "I know people often think of me
as obtuse — do not deny it," he challenged as Darcy
opened his mouth to speak. "To be fair, I often am.
I am not so quick to catch on to things as some,
but I am not oblivious to the world around me. I do
spend time in observation and contemplation." He
smirked. "Not so much as you, my friend, but I do
practice the skills occasionally."

Darcy chuckled.

"You know I care for Georgiana, though not as
my sister would wish for me to care for her," Bingley said.

Again, Darcy chuckled, and Bingley joined him.
They knew that Caroline wished for not just one
connection to the Darcy family through marrying
Darcy herself. She also wanted her brother to
marry Darcy's sister. To her, there was no better

way to ensure they had risen above their roots in trade than to secure ties to the aristocracy and ancient lands and money.

"I care for her as a brother might care for her. I would not wish to see her harmed in any fashion." Bingley came back to where Darcy still sat swirling and occasionally sipping his drink. "She still feels the weight of disappointing you, Darcy. I can see it in her eyes when she looks at you when you are unaware." Darcy had shared with him about Georgiana's ordeal with Wickham at Ramsgate.

"But she has not disappointed me. I have failed her." Darcy's brows furrowed as he shook his head.

"Yet, she perceives she has disappointed you, and it still plays upon her spirit. Imagine how her spirit would suffer if she were to learn you had given up happiness for her. You know as well as I that she would never be happy no matter the match you might make for her." He shrugged. "And what match will you make for her? Will it be one of duty and obligation, or do you wish for her to find felicity and love? And with time, might you not grow to resent the fact that you gave up the possibility of your own felicity for your sister?"

Darcy gaped at his friend. "I had not thought of

it in those terms. But, I fear, it does not matter. Miss Elizabeth would not have me anyway.

"Why would she not have you? I see no reason for her to reject you." Bingley knew he was close to securing a solution. He had learned from his father that there were always a few nagging details which threatened to sink any negotiation. Hopefully, this obstacle would be easily overcome, although, with Darcy, even a small barrier could become nearly insurmountable when he was in a dour state of mind, such as he was this evening.

"She believes George Wickham." Darcy drained the remaining liquid from his glass and placed it firmly on the table next to him. "Which means he has once again stolen from me that which is dear."

"He has not," Bingley refuted. "He did not succeed with Georgiana, and he will not succeed with Miss Elizabeth either."

Darcy's jaw clenched as he shook his head. "He has already influenced her against me."

"How do you know?" With any luck, there would be a great leap that had been made by his friend, who could be overly pessimistic about things at times and see one small error as the ruin of a project.

"She questioned me about Wickham at your ball."

Bingley leaned back in his chair and bit his cheeks to keep from smiling with satisfaction. He had heard about Miss Elizabeth's questioning as Darcy had vented his frustration on an innocent set of billiard balls. It might be challenging to overcome the obstacles of George Wickham and Miss Elizabeth's poor opinion of Darcy, but from Bingley's position, when considering the whole scheme of Miss Elizabeth and George Wickham, there was at least one way in which he knew he could very likely prod Darcy into action.

"Ah," Bingley began, "so that is the real reason why you were in such a rush to return to London. You were unwilling to fight for Miss Elizabeth. Do you really think of yourself so meanly when compared to him? I must say it is rather startling that you do."

Darcy bristled as Bingley knew he would. Not even the staid Mr. Darcy could keep from reacting with displeasure when his masculine sensibilities were challenged. In fact, Bingley knew that Darcy's sense of honour was likely more honed and, therefore, more easily provoked than most gentlemen in the higher echelons of society.

"I do not trust him to behave in a way which will not bring harm to all those I care about." Darcy's voice was satisfyingly close to a growl. "It is safer for her if I do not fight him. He could not only harm her but her family as well."

Bingley shook his head. He knew that his friend would not allow any about whom he cared to be placed in harm's way and would sacrifice himself to see them safe, but his logic, in this case, was sadly lacking. "Have you listened to yourself?"

Darcy's brows furrowed in question.

"Tell me. Exactly how is Miss Elizabeth safer with him than with you?"

Darcy huffed in disbelief, and Bingley waited patiently for him to explain.

"He will leave her alone as long as he does not think I am interested in her," Darcy explained. "Why do you suppose he singled her out to befriend after our meeting on the street in Meryton? She was acquainted with me, and my shock upon seeing him may have left me unable to hide my jealousy. Wickham knows me well. He would not miss such a thing. However, she has no money to tempt him into anything more than a light flirtation, and he would never risk being tied to a woman that would not provide amply for his expenses."

Bingley shrugged. "True, but I still do not see how she is safer. What if she does lose her heart to him? While he may not marry a penniless woman, he is not above taking the little she has to offer." His brows rose as he gave his friend a pointed look.

Darcy groaned and ran his hands through his hair. "Surely, she would not succumb to his charms. She is far too intelligent."

"And Georgiana is not?"

Darcy was on his feet and pacing. "What do I do? Ride back to Longbourn and tell her stories of his past?" He sighed and shook his head at such a foolish idea. "She does not like me. I am sure I cannot convince her of his failings. I will only look like a vengeful fool."

"So, do not convince her," Bingley replied. "She has a sister in town, and there is always the possibility of a well-worded letter placed in the hands of a man she respects such as her father or Sir William. I am sure Wickham has amassed a fair number of debts within the past months. Let her see his character for what it is. She is intelligent. She will see the error in her judgment."

Darcy stopped mid-stride and turned to look at his friend. Relicf suffused his features. "Bingley, I do not give you enough credit for your depth of understanding. You are positively wise tonight. Where do you suggest we start? With Miss Bennet?"

Bingley chuckled softly at his friend's exuberance — a word not often associated with the man standing before him. "As much as I would love to start with a visit to Miss Bennet, I rather think a visit to your cousin would be better."

Darcy's cousin, Colonel Richard Fitzwilliam, was well-known and respected by many. He also happened to despise Wickham. Both were items that could help their cause.

"Perhaps Richard could have some influence with Wickham's commanding officer? Colonel Forster may wish to know of Wickham's tendencies to gamble and dally with the ladies — not all turn a blind eye to such behaviors, you know. You do not even have to mention Miss Elizabeth to Richard. You just have to let him know where Wickham is. I doubt your cousin needs any further incentive to make the man's life as miserable as possible."

Darcy's lips curled in a knowing smile. "Richard would need very little incentive to relieve Wickham of his life. If you will allow me, I will send a note to him now, letting him know I need to speak with him."

Bingley motioned to his desk. "Whatever I have is at your disposal."

Chapter 3

"Darcy," Bingley said as Darcy finished his missive to Colonel Fitzwilliam, "perhaps you could help me with a little problem?"

Darcy glanced up from the paper he was folding and preparing to seal. "Anything."

"My sister..."

"Except that," Darcy interrupted with a chuckle.

Bingley shook his head. "I would not foist her on you. If that were my intention, I would have done it long ago instead of suffering through these years with her airs."

Darcy inclined his head in acceptance. He was thankful his friend had the good sense not to throw his sister in Darcy's path. Caroline Bingley was not the sort of lady that he had ever considered. She was too... His brows furrowed, what was she exactly? Devious, practiced, lacking in warmth? Any of those would do, he supposed. Put simply; she did not possess a nature that appealed to him.

"I do not know what to do about her hiding Miss Bennet's call from me," Bingley continued. "You know I am not the best at knowing how to deal with Caroline." He sighed. "I wish she would just marry and be someone else's problem."

Darcy lifted a brow. "You care for her," he reminded him.

Bingley shrugged. "Not so much at this moment as I did before I knew she was trying to keep Miss Bennet away from me. I would rather fob her off onto the first chap to seem welcoming than have to keep her and act appropriately."

"You would not fob her off on the first chap," Darcy contradicted with a smile. His friend really did care for both of his sisters, no matter how much they annoyed him. "You would see her well-settled, at least."

Bingley blew out a resigned breath. "Then what do I do?"

"Nothing," Darcy replied. "Call on Miss Bennet." He rose and returned to the group of chairs where he and Bingley had been sitting before and where Bingley was now. "Tell your sister nothing about it. Continue as if nothing has changed."

Bingley's eyes grew wide. "Is that not rather a lot of disguise?"

Darcy pondered the question for a moment and then shrugged. "Tell her if you must or if she asks, but it will not aid your cause."

"But you hate –"

"Normally, yes," Darcy interrupted, "however, it seems necessary at the moment."

Bingley's brows furrowed as he nodded his agreement.

"I will even go with you to call on Miss Bennet," Darcy offered.

"You would do that?" Bingley's eyes were wide in surprise. "Her relations are in Cheapside."

Darcy shook his head. "No, they are near Cheapside," he corrected. "On Gracechurch Street, if I am not mistaken."

"That is well-removed from Grosvenor Square," Bingley cautioned.

"I know where it is," Darcy retorted, "and I am not so priggish as you seem to think."

Bingley shrugged and gave his friend a look that said he was not entirely convinced that travelling to that portion of London would not be a trial. "If you are certain, I would be happy for the company."

"Then, it is settled. We will call on Miss Bennet together."

Bingley smiled as understanding dawned on him. "You wish for her to write to her sister about your visit."

"Of course." Having Jane write to Elizabeth about the fact that he had brought Bingley to Jane and had visited her relations in Gracechurch Street would have to earn him some small amount of merit, would it not?

"Very well," said Bingley, leaning forward with eagerness, "do you know exactly where her relations live?"

Darcy shook his head. "I only know it is on Gracechurch Street."

Bingley scowled for a moment, his brows furrowed in thought. He took the letter Darcy was tapping on the arm of his chair and went to the door.

"Jenkins," he called down the hall and then waited for his butler to join him. "Has my sister received any letters from Gracechurch Street?"

Jenkins was a most fastidious butler, and if a piece of correspondence had entered the house, he would know when it arrived, to whom it was addressed, and from whence it had come.

"Yes, sir, she has."

"Do you remember the number in the direction?"

"Of course, sir. It was eighteen."

"Eighteen Gracechurch Street?"

"Yes, sir. Will there be anything else?"

"Would you see that this is delivered?" Bingley handed Darcy's message to him.

"Tonight, sir?"

"Yes, as soon as can be managed."

Bingley closed the door behind Jenkins and rejoined Darcy.

"So, tomorrow, you will accompany me on a social call?" He could not help the smirk that he wore.

"Happily," Darcy answered.

Bingley chortled. "Happily? I repeat, this is a social call, and you will be required to be affable."

Darcy shook his head and smiled. "I know that such a thing is not my strongest suit, but I have a vested interest in your success. For, it seems, I am most anxious to be allowed the chance to disappoint my family's expectations."

As Darcy was speaking, the door of the study was flung open and Darcy's cousin, Colonel Richard Fitzwilliam entered, followed by a flustered Jenkins.

"I am sorry, sir," the butler apologized. "I tried to get him to wait."

Bingley chuckled. "We are all sorry at one time or another for Richard, Jenkins. Think nothing of it." Bingley clapped Richard on the shoulder. "I did not think you would receive Darcy's message so soon."

"Message?" Richard questioned. " I did not receive a message. I stopped by Darcy's, and his butler told me that he was here, so I came. What message was I to receive? Does it have anything to do with my cousin disappointing his family?" Richard smiled wickedly at Darcy.

"This is why one waits to be announced," grumbled Darcy. "There are things that you are not supposed to hear."

At that moment, Jenkins re-entered the room. "A message for you, sir." He bowed, handed an envelope to Richard, and was gone.

Richard broke the seal and scanned the contents of Darcy's message, looking up from it in surprise. "You wish to discuss an old acquaintance?"

"Yes," Bingley took out a third glass and filled it with an ample amount of brandy. "It seems that an old acquaintance of yours has surfaced in Meryton, which is near my estate in Hertfordshire." He handed the glass to Richard. "You may wish to drink this first."

Richard eyed Bingley and Darcy suspiciously. "And who might that be?"

"Wickham," said Darcy.

Richard muttered and took a healthy gulp of his drink.

"Bingley's neighbour has five daughters, and he is concerned for their safety." Darcy felt his ears warm at the half-truth. Hiding Bingley's call on Miss Bennet call from Caroline gave him no qualms but hiding anything from Richard always did, and while it was accurate that Bingley wished to see the Bennets safe, he was not the only one who wished it.

"Five daughters?" Richard whistled softly. "And would one of these be your new angel?" he asked

Bingley. "You do still find an angel in every town, do you not?"

"If things go well," Darcy answered before Bingley could, "I think this may be Bingley's last angel."

Richard let out another slow whistle. "She must be quite the lady."

Bingley grinned, utterly undaunted by Richard's teasing tone. "She is," he said, "and she has four sisters that need protection from Wickham."

Richard tipped his head and looked from Bingley to Darcy and back. "Your angel has been seen in company with you and Darcy?"

Bingley nodded. "As have certain of her sisters." Bingley winked slyly at Richard.

Darcy groaned inwardly as he shook his head. Of course, Bingley would not keep that information to himself.

Richard's brows rose as an impish grin spread across his face. "Has my cousin singled out any sister in particular?"

"Yes, your cousin has," Darcy answered. There seemed no need to try to deny it. Richard would know the truth and to tell him directly was better than to be taunted by both his cousin and Bingley. "Miss Elizabeth Bennet."

"Miss Bennet's next youngest sister," Bingley added.

Richard rubbed his knuckles against his jaw. "And Wickham knows this?"

Darcy nodded. "I believe so. Therefore, we have decided that Bingley will inform Miss Bennet that Wickham is not to be trusted with the hope that she will then impart this information to her sisters; although, I am not sure the information will be immediately accepted by all." He shifted in his seat. "Bingley thought that perhaps you could inform Colonel Forster of Wickham's penchant for cards and women. He has been in the area long enough to have accrued a fair amount of debt, both with the merchants of the area and other members of the regiment. Your word would go a long way in helping me refute the stories that I am sure he has been spreading about me."

Richard blew out a breath. "Miss Elizabeth believes Wickham?"

Darcy nodded slowly. He wished it was not true, but it was.

"Which means she is set against you, and you are besotted with her enough to consider going against familial duty." Richard surmised.

"I would not say besotted," retorted Darcy.

"I would," Bingley muttered.

Richard threw back his head and laughed. "It is about time."

"Why were you looking for me tonight?" Darcy asked before Richard could continue down a road that Darcy was certain he did not wish to have traversed.

Richard lifted his glass. "A drink, a game of billiards, some conversation, and a comfortable bed."

Darcy's lips twitched. "There are beds at Matlock House that are quite comfortable. In fact, there is one there reserved for you."

"There is also one at Darcy House." He consumed what remained in his glass. "However, your home lacks one thing that my parents' house does not."

"Your mother?" Darcy asked with a grin.

"Precisely. I have no desire to hear her concerns regarding my lack of a wife." He placed his glass on the table next to Darcy's and lay a hand on his cousin's shoulder for a moment. "If you will forget family expectations and for once pursue your own happiness, then, I might be inspired to do the same, and my mother will be delighted."

He continued as Darcy rose from his chair, ready to take his leave, "Do you know how many times I have heard Father and Mother speaking about how they wish to see you happy?" He chuckled as Darcy shook his head. "Neither do they, but it is a great number, to be sure. They will be pleased for you. It is only Aunt Catherine who might pose an issue. But then, when is she not an issue?"

Darcy and Bingley both chuckled along with Richard. Lady Catherine was known for voicing her opinion about many things quite loudly, and the more her opinion was ignored, as it often was by her brother, the more vocal she would become until eventually, her arguments would expire in a huff.

"It is not only Lady Catherine about whom you need worry," said Bingley. "I have a sister who is not easily dissuaded and is intent on securing Pemberley."

Richard shook his head. "Is she still at that?"

"Stubborn, is she not?" Bingley said as he nodded his answer to Richard's question.

"Extremely," Darcy muttered.

Richard clapped him on the shoulder. "We

should take our leave unless you wish to encounter her tonight."

"You will contact Colonel Forster?" Bingley asked as they moved into the corridor.

"I will send him a letter tomorrow, and I am certain Darcy will see that it travels by express?"

Darcy rolled his eyes. If there was one thing that Richard was good at, aside from his role as colonel, it was weaseling out of extra expenditures. For one who had grown up in a house filled with plenty, he had a strong miserly bent as well as an eye for investment to increase his holdings. A strategic mind, he called it and said it was what made him proficient in his profession.

"I will call for you tomorrow before I head toward Cheapside to call on Miss Bennet," Bingley said to Darcy as they reached the front door.

"Cheapside?" Richard whistled low. "You do mean to disappoint the family." He laughed and slapped his cousin on the back.

"It is where her uncle lives. She is a gentleman's daughter," Darcy argued.

Richard moved down the steps briskly and prepared to mount his horse. "You may tell me all her excellent qualities over a game of billiards." He swung up into his saddle and with a salute was off.

"You know you will have to tell him everything, do you not?" Bingley asked.

Darcy nodded. Along with having a miserly streak, Richard Fitzwilliam was also persistent, and much like a starving dog might latch onto a piece of meat and refuse to let go, if there was something that Darcy's cousin wished to know, he was going to discover it, using whatever means he could. "As long as he lends his help, I will bare my very soul."

"Thank you," Bingley said as Darcy climbed into his carriage, "for telling me about Miss Bennet's call and all."

Darcy leaned forward in his seat so that he could see out the door to where his friend stood. "It is I who should thank you — first, for not tossing me out and, then, for helping me to see reason."

"My happiness could not be complete without yours," Bingley said. "And I promise you, we will find ourselves happy, in spite of my sister."

Chapter 4

Darcy and Bingley stood just inside the foyer of a neat but modest home on Gracechurch Street, waiting for their cards to be presented to the mistress of the home and her niece.

"The Gardiners do not appear to be destitute or even wanting," Bingley whispered. "This paper is new." He nodded toward the wall. "Caroline has admired it and has begged me to allow her to redecorate the front sitting room with it. However, I prefer paint over flowers." He pursed his lips as he studied the paper on the wall. "Unless of course my wife prefers flowers, and then I shall prefer them as well."

Darcy chuckled. "I have not considered my preference one way or the other. I simply wish my surroundings to look..." His brow furrowed as he thought of how best to describe his taste in decor.

It really was not something he considered often. He knew what he liked and what he did not, but he had not put significant effort into deciding how he would decorate a home. His mother had done that sort of thing, and now, if a space needed refreshing, he simply deferred to the opinion of either Georgiana or Lady Matlock. He shrugged. "I prefer my rooms to be welcoming and not garish, homely and not ostentatious."

"Which is why my sister should not be allowed to decorate your home or mine," Bingley said with a smirk. "Are you prepared to see if it is possible to convince a Bennet lady to take on such a task?" he whispered as they followed behind the maid who directed them to the sitting room on their right.

They had discussed how they would approach this interview as they had travelled together today. It was decided that the folly of both Caroline and Darcy should be broached directly as neither gentleman wished to be left wondering as to their position in hoping to attain their happiness.

"Mr. Bingley, Mr. Darcy, it is a pleasure to meet you," a lady, dressed in the current fashion of the day and appearing to be no older than Darcy, if she was even that, greeted them as they entered the room.

"The pleasure is ours, Mrs. Gardiner," Bingley said as he took her hand and bowed over it. "It is a pleasure that should have been ours much earlier had we known your niece was in town."

Mrs. Gardiner barely contained a grin. "That is a welcome sentiment, is it not, Jane?" she asked as she extended her hand to Mr. Darcy.

"Indeed, it is," Jane replied.

"Please, be seated while I arrange for tea." Mrs. Gardiner slipped behind Mr. Darcy and into the hall for a moment but was back before either gentleman had settled into his chair completely.

To Darcy, she rather flitted about like a bird, happily doing all that needed to be done. She tucked away some material that lay on a work table and pulled the table out to be used, he assumed, for the tea service. Then, she perched lightly in her chair, looking at ease but ready to fly away again if she should be needed for something.

"Mr. Bingley, I understand that you have been considering an estate in Hertfordshire," Mrs. Gardiner began, directing the conversation to exactly where Darcy and Bingley had hoped it would eventually fall. "Will you return to it once the season draws to a close? I understand you are in town because you have a sister in need of a husband."

Darcy found the way the lady's lips twitched with amusement to be telling of what she had likely heard about Miss Bingley, and the way that her eyes danced reminded him of Elizabeth. He was certain he would enjoy having this woman's acquaintance.

"Of course, you are also unmarried," she continued, "so I suppose you might also be looking for a wife while squiring your sister to this function and that."

Even Darcy could not mistake the meaning of Mrs. Gardiner's words when accompanied by the pointed look she gave Bingley. It was apparent that Mrs. Gardiner was not the sort of lady to play games but came directly to the point, and that fact made him like her all the more.

"I should not say it, but I will be beyond elated when my sister finally marries," Bingley admitted. "She is no small trial."

"Oh, we all have relations like that," Mrs. Gardiner said with a grin. "Some are born to us while others are attached by marriage. I do hope she finds a husband who does not add to your affliction."

Bingley chuckled. "I most heartily hope the same."

"And what of you, Mr. Bingley? Has the season been kind to you — aside from the trials of a sibling?"

Determined and not to be thwarted in her pursuit — Darcy added these qualities to the list of items that recommended Mrs. Gardiner to him.

Bingley held Mrs. Gardiner's gaze. "Not until this moment," he said before darting his eyes toward Jane and returning them to her aunt and adding, "I hope."

"Very well said," Mrs. Gardiner replied with no small amount of approval in her voice. "We had heard you had intentions of a marriage in the future when a particular lady was finally presented to society." She stood to pour the tea as the maid laid out the service for her.

"You speak of my sister."

Mrs. Gardiner acknowledged the veracity of Darcy's words with a nod of her head.

"Neither Bingley nor I have ever harboured such a wish for any such joining of our families."

Bingley gave his fervent agreement. "I assure you that I view Miss Darcy as nothing more than the sister of a very good friend. If our families are ever joined, it shall not be through either of our sisters." He turned to Jane. "I must apologize for the actions of my sister. I only learned last evening that you were in town and that is only because Darcy told me."

Jane looked between the men in confusion.

"Miss Bingley told me of your call when I stopped to deliver something to Bingley yesterday afternoon." Darcy accepted a cup of tea from Mrs. Gardiner and then began his painful confession. "She thought I would be delighted about how she had snubbed you. I was not, of course, although I admit to not remonstrating her for her actions but only accepting her account and fleeing as quickly as I could."

Bingley chuckled. "You must forgive him for that. Darcy knows my sister's intentions in regard to his marital state and has no desire to encourage those attentions or to find himself unwarily caught in a trap from which his honour will not allow him to escape."

"You do not like Miss Bingley?" Jane asked Darcy in surprise.

Darcy grimaced and looked at Bingley apologetically. "Not particularly. However, there was a reason for her to think I would find her actions towards you acceptable, and for that, I must apologize. You see, I supported Miss Bingley's desire to leave Netherfield and persuade her brother not to return." He closed his eyes and shook his head in self-remonstration. "I abhor disguise, Miss Bennet, and yet, I prevaricated most grievously. I agreed with Miss Bingley that a connection between her family and yours would not be beneficial to her brother."

He stood and placed his untouched tea on the tea tray. He knew admission of his failings would be difficult, but to see the pain in the eyes of a woman as kind and sweet as he knew Miss Bennet to be made the task far harder than he had imagined.

"I will admit to having certain reservations about your family." He grimaced. "They have nothing to do with your ties to trade. They are — were solely based on what I have perceived to be improper behavior." He shook his head again.

"Not even I can deny how arrogant that sounds." Indeed, as he said the words here, in the sitting room, standing before both Miss Bennet and her relation, the words sounded like those of a pretentious fool. "Please forgive me."

He drew a breath. He needed to complete his admission of guilt, no matter how painful it might be to do so. "I worked to keep Mr. Bingley from returning to Netherfield as he wished." He smiled sadly at Jane whose eyes had grown wide at his comment. "He wished to return to you. However, I had made a promise to remain with him at his estate until he had decided on either purchasing or moving on and then, if he purchased, until he had enough knowledge to stand on his own as master of his own domain. However, I could not return." He shook his head slowly as he returned to his seat. "I simply could not be there."

"I should not have allowed myself to be persuaded," Bingley said softly as Darcy retreated into his chair to allow Bingley to make his own apology to Miss Bennet.

"No," Jane agreed, "you should not have."

"Was it an unpardonable error?" Bingley's heart thumped wildly, and his palms became moist while drawing a breath became something about which he needed to think. How he would survive a negative response without making a complete cake of himself, he was uncertain.

Jane's cheeks grew rosy, and she took a slow sip from her cup. Then, as she returned her cup to her saucer with only a small clatter, she answered. "It is only unpardonable if your intentions in calling today are less than sincere or if you should be so easily persuaded once again."

"I promise my intentions are both sincere and unwavering," Bingley replied, passing his cup to Darcy. "I fear I will drop this if I must hold it any longer." He rubbed his hands on his breeches. "If you will allow me, Miss Bennet, I will request an interview with your uncle to gain his blessing in your father's stead to court you. I know this is not exactly the most fitting setting for such a discussion. I should have asked to speak to you in private. However, I came today determined to discover if I had any hope of winning you, and I am willing to openly suffer any humiliation my offer may bring." He smiled sheepishly. "Although I would be lying if I said I did not hope to avoid the humiliation of rejection."

"You may speak to my uncle," Jane said with a smile.

Bingley grasped Jane's hand which was not holding her cup and lifting it, kissed it. "Thank you," he whispered, returning her smile.

"My husband will not be home for many hours," Mrs. Gardiner said. "He is to dine with an associate this evening."

"Tomorrow would be soon enough," Bingley replied. "Unless it would not be too offensive for me to visit his place of business today."

Mrs. Gardiner chuckled. "You do not do things by halves, do you, Mr. Bingley?"

"Not when it is of such importance as this," Bingley replied with a smile. "Now, if you were to ask me to muck out the stables, I might not be so eager."

"I shall ask you to do no such thing." Mrs. Gardiner's left brow rose with an impertinence that reminded Darcy once again of Elizabeth. "However, there are four children in the nursery, and I would not be above shuffling one or more of them off on you so that both their nurse and I might have a nice quiet cup of tea and a read."

Bingley shrugged and settled back into his chair.

"I am fond of both children and toys, especially if there might be a tin of biscuits involved."

"Oh, boys and their biscuits!" Mrs. Gardiner cried. "My youngest son is forever attempting to sneak an extra treat when his nurse's back is turned." She chuckled. "He is only two, so, though I reprimand, it is forgivable." She held out a plate of almond cakes to Bingley.

"Mr. Darcy," she began as Bingley selected two cakes from the plate, causing her to smile. "You are like John," she said to Bingley before turning back to Darcy. "You said you could not return to Netherfield, and I admit to being curious as to the cause of your reluctance — nay — refusal to return." She offered him an almond cake and refused to move from her spot until he had taken one. Then, she gathered his cup from the tea tray and returned that to him as well. "I will not have you leave without refreshment," she said kindly before returning to her seat. "Would I be correct in assuming it had something to do with another one of my nieces?"

Darcy washed down his bite of cake with some tea. "Yes," he replied simply.

Chapter 5

"Were you much attached to Lizzy?" Jane asked, causing Darcy's eyes to widen in surprise.

The Miss Bennet he was witnessing today in this drawing room clashed with the one he remembered from his time in Hertfordshire. This Miss Bennet was much bolder. However, from the pink that stained her cheeks and the way her eyes did not hold his for long before dropping away, he knew that the effort was not without cost.

"Surprisingly, yes," he admitted. "Although I did not realize just how much until I returned to town and could not rid myself of her memory."

"She likes you," Jane's voice was no more than a whisper.

"I am sorry to disagree with you, Miss Bennet, but your sister most certainly does not like me," Darcy returned.

"Oh, no," Mrs. Gardiner said, "our Lizzy is quite taken with you. She just does not realize it."

For the first time since his arrival, Darcy saw the woman relax into her chair and take a leisurely sip of her tea rather than the quick ones she had taken thus far.

"You will have to explain that to me," Darcy said. "I was left with the distinct impression that she did not approve of me any more than I approved of such a connection at that time."

"How will your family receive her?" Mrs. Gardiner asked.

Darcy shook his head and shrugged. "I do not know, but first –"

"Do you love her?" Mrs. Gardiner interrupted.

Darcy drew a deep breath and released it as he nodded his head. "But I do not see how –"

"Good," Mrs. Gardiner interrupted again.

It appeared that the lady was determined to be the only one asking questions and directing the conversation, so Darcy leaned back and waited expectantly.

"No more protests, Mr. Darcy?"

The familiar twinkle had returned to Mrs. Gardiner's eyes, causing the right side of Darcy's mouth tipped up in a half smile. "You are very much like her," he commented.

Mrs. Gardiner finished the tea in her cup and placed it to the side. "I cannot deny that. However, the fact that you have recognized it speaks to how much you must admire her to have noticed such a thing. Tell me, because my curiosity must be satisfied: what makes you say that Elizabeth and I are alike?"

Darcy tipped his head. "You would leave your children in the care of Bingley to have a cup of tea and a read. Therefore, I assume you enjoy reading as much as she does."

With a tip of her head, Mrs. Gardiner accepted his statement as true.

"You are determined and unafraid to speak your mind. You challenged both me and Bingley."

"One of my faults," Mrs. Gardiner said with a smile.

"No, I do not find it to be a fault. I prefer directness to prevarication and pandering." He watched the light dance in the eyes of the woman before him. "Her eyes sparkle and dance just as yours do, and her brow raises in much the same fashion as yours is now." A smile spread across his face. "And, her lips purse and twitch just like that when she is trying to contain her amusement."

Mrs. Gardiner clapped her hands in delight. "Oh, you do love her!"

Darcy nodded. "But –" He stopped as Mrs. Gardiner held up a hand.

"She would not dislike you so much as she does if she did not like you."

Darcy's brows furrowed. How could dislike equate to like? "I beg your pardon?"

Bingley chuckled.

"Do you understand her meaning?" Darcy asked his friend.

"I think I might," Bingley replied. "The lady doth protest too much, me thinks."

Darcy's eyes grew wide. "Shakespeare?"

"I said I read occasionally," Bingley retorted.

"He has the right of it," said Mrs. Gardiner, "does he not, Jane?"

Jane nodded. "Oh, indeed. Lizzy avows her dislike far too much for it not to indicate how much she wishes for your good opinion."

Darcy's brows furrowed as he shook his head trying to rid himself of the perplexity such statements brought. "But she has my good opinion; she does not have to wish for it."

"Oh, she knows she has your *tolerably* good opinion," Mrs. Gardiner said as she rose and gathered empty cups. Both of her brows rose as she took Mr. Darcy's cup from him. "I am afraid she heard your comment at the assembly. In fact, I am quite certain everyone who knows and is close to Lizzy has heard your comment from the assembly. I had it in a letter not two days after it was spoken."

Darcy blew out a breath and closed his eyes for a moment. "Then, if she is so set against me, do I have any hope?"

Mrs. Gardiner placed the cups she held on the tea tray and then, as she crossed the room to summon someone to clear the things away, she stopped and lay a hand on Darcy's shoulder much like Richard's mother would at times when attempting to reassure him of something.

"Hope is not lost until she is married to someone other than you. Until that time, we must not faint." She gave his shoulder a pat and then rang for the maid.

"Now, we must decide how to proceed," she said as she returned to her seat. "I am not a matchmaker, mind you. However, I do long to see my nieces well-settled."

Her smile and accompanying laugh were infectious, filling the room with a lightness it had not had for several minutes.

"I might be able to persuade her to visit," Mrs. Gardiner said. "And then you can call just as you are now, and she will see that you are not as she thinks." She winked. "I will be certain to sing your praises if she should disparage. An unhappy Lizzy is known to allow her tongue to get the better of her good sense. Aside from getting Elizabeth here and allowing Mr. Darcy to confuse and then charm her, are there any other contentious items that need our forethought?"

"I am positive she has heard some very disparaging stories about me," Darcy said. "Mr. Wickham is not a champion of the Darcy name. I am right, am I not?" he asked as he noted how Jane drew her lower lip between her teeth and dropped her gaze.

Jane nodded.

Darcy shook his head. "I cannot tell you all that has passed between us, but I can assure you that it is not Mr. Wickham's normal wont to speak truthfully regarding how things now stand between us. He is not to be trusted."

"Indeed, he is not," Bingley affirmed gravely.

"I have not believed him," Jane said with a smile. "He spoke too freely with an acquaintance of a short duration. I told Lizzy to be wary, and I do not think she is completely convinced by his words. Did she not ask you about him at the ball?"

"She did."

"If you would but answer her, her opinion might be swayed. I know you could not on a dance floor, but she is not thinking clearly. You have unsettled her." Jane paused and then continued. "There is, however, one item about which I should like to ask."

"Whatever you wish to know, Miss Bennet," Darcy offered.

"Are you betrothed?"

Darcy shook his head. "No matter how much my aunt insists that it happens, I am not betrothed to her daughter, nor will I ever be betrothed to her daughter. It will come as a great disappointment to her, I suppose," he added sardonically.

Jane's broad smile at the comment was, Darcy recognized, the equivalent of another more vocal lady's chuckle. He was beginning to recognize in the short time they had spent together this afternoon that her emotions were conveyed in small, subtle ways that required greater attention than he had given them in Meryton. She was not a fawning lady of the ton but a gracious and demure lady of quality. His friend would do well to secure her.

"My mother was quite disappointed with Elizabeth in such a fashion recently."

"I beg your pardon?" Darcy asked as his heart began racing and his stomach twisted. Wickham would not offer for a lady of little wealth — not even to spite Darcy. Would he?

"Mr. Collins, our cousin, made an offer. My mother was beside herself demanding that Elizabeth retract her refusal. The whole house was in an uproar until Mr. Collins removed himself to Lucas Lodge, where he found a lady who was more amenable to his offer."

"Mr. Collins? The large man with an excess of words and an inability to dance without injuring his partner?"

At this, Jane actually giggled as she nodded. "Yes, that Mr. Collins. A most ridiculous match, is it not?"

"Indeed," Darcy muttered. How would anyone with half a morsel of sense think that a lady as intelligent and quick-witted as Elizabeth would make a good match for a bumbling fool like Mr. Collins? The idea was far beyond ridiculous. It was ludicrous, and he was happy that it appeared Elizabeth's refusal had stood.

"He married Miss Lucas," Mrs. Gardiner added. "But it is not Mr. Collins we wish to see married, now is it?"

Darcy found himself chuckling at her pointed look.

"No," he replied. He hoped to see both Bingley and himself happily leg-shackled before his annual trip to Rosings at Easter, where he would both have to endure his aunt and Mr. Collins. A smile settled firmly on his lips. Perhaps if he were fortunate to secure a bride before Easter, he would not be required to visit Rosings at all since his aunt's displeasure would undoubtedly take some time to quell.

"Do you think you can persuade Miss Elizabeth to visit soon?" Darcy asked. "It may take some time for me to convince her that I am not so unworthy as I portrayed myself."

"Oh, I should think she would be very willing to visit soon. I imagine that there is a fair bit of unpleasantness to be endured at home since her mother is displeased to know that Longbourn is not to fall to one of her daughters but to Miss Lucas. I will write today, and perhaps Jane will add a note of invitation as well?" She cast a questioning look at her niece.

"Please tell her that I came to call," Bingley said as he rose to leave. "And that it was at Darcy's insistence. In fact, it is through Darcy that I learned of Miss Bennet's being in town. That should do some good in shedding a bit of a rosy glow on my friend, should it not?" He looked from one lady to the other.

"It will," Jane said quietly.

Mrs. Gardiner, followed by Jane, rose to see their guests out of the room, and after a few words of parting and Bingley managing to get the directions to Mr. Gardiner's warehouse, the two gentlemen stepped out onto the street, feeling very hopeful.

Chapter 6

"Gentlemen," Mr. Gardiner rose and greeted the two men who entered his office. "How might I be of service to you today?" He made a sweeping motion to the chairs that stood before a desk, covered with a few small boxes on one end and a stack of account books and papers on the other. He tucked his ink and pen away and straightened the few documents that were before him into a neat pile.

Darcy noted the emblem that graced the tops of several of the papers and was stamped on the side of one box that was facing him. Though the lady who looked at him from that box did not always appear in the same dress — what lady did — there was no mistaking her identity. Mr. Gardiner was, apparently, a member of the Mercers' Company.

"We have just come from calling at your home," Bingley began.

Mr. Gardiner, a good-natured-looking gentleman of no more than five and thirty, leaned back in his chair, a small smile playing at the corners of his mouth. "Indeed? I hope you were not too disappointed to find I was not home." His lips twitched with barely contained amusement.

Bingley laughed. "Seeing as my goal was to call on your niece, I was not disappointed in the least."

A grin spread across Mr. Gardiner's face. "I had hoped you were calling for her and not me," he replied. "I also hope you are calling on me now because of her." He tipped his head and smiled. "I am not a man to shake the bushes in hopes that for which I am searching falls out. I prefer to come to the point where it is prudent." He propped his elbows on the arms of his chair and clasped his hands in front of him. "We have heard much about both of you gentlemen." He grimaced. "I wish I could say it has all been good, but I am not the sort to bear false tales."

"Well-deserved criticism," Darcy assured him, causing the gentleman's eyebrows to raise.

"Indeed?"

Darcy nodded. "I have made my full confession of folly to your wife."

"As have I," Bingley added.

"And was your folly forgiven?" Gardiner's eyes shifted from Bingley to Darcy and back.

"Yes," Bingley replied with a grin.

"By your wife and Miss Bennet," Darcy added. "And I hope, eventually, to be forgiven by Miss Elizabeth as well."

"Hmm," Gardiner muttered as he nodded his head in a pleased fashion. "I am certain my wife will apprise me of the details when I return home this evening."

"I am certain she will," Darcy agreed.

"So, you do not dislike our Lizzy, then?"

The smile he wore told Darcy he knew the answer to that question, but Darcy answered anyway. "I like her very much."

Gardiner chuckled and turned to Bingley. "And I assume you like Jane?"

Bingley's cheeks grew noticeably red. It was one of the hazards of having a fair complexion. "I love her," Bingley answered, "and I would like to have permission to court her."

"Done," Gardiner said with a sharp nod of his head.

"Done?" Bingley repeated. "Do you not wish to

ask me my intentions or about why I have not called before now or ... or ... or ... something?"

Gardiner chuckled and shook his head. "My niece is not foolish. I trust her judgment and that of my wife. You would not be here if you had not gotten past Addie and been sent to me; therefore, you have passed the only test I require."

"But what of my wealth and standing?" Bingley questioned.

"You have five thousand a year, your father was in trade — something that does not concern me in the least — and you are planning to purchase an estate eventually — although might I caution you not to consider Netherfield. Is there anything else I should know?"

Bingley shook his head. "No, I believe that covers the high points. Why should I not consider Netherfield?"

"You have met my sister, have you not?"

"Mrs. Bennet?"

Gardiner nodded. "In my experience, she does not improve with acquaintance, but then, she is my sister. However, I know she will be on your doorstep every second day at least." He grimaced. "I was not blessed with sensible sisters."

"Neither was I, " Bingley commiserated.

Gardiner shifted forward in his chair. "It is best to see them married and well-settled as soon as possible and at a distance that allows them to grow dear to you." He winked. "A half-day's journey is the least I would recommend. Now, was there anything else I could do for you, gentlemen?"

"There was a matter of some delicacy that we had hoped to discuss with you at some point," Darcy said.

Mr. Gardiner pulled his watch from his pocket and after giving it a quick glance, said, "I have an hour before I have to be anywhere, and I would welcome the diversion from my books."

"Have you heard of Mr. Wickham?" Darcy asked.

Mr. Gardiner nodded. "Elizabeth has mentioned him in her letters, and Jane has told us some about him."

"He is not what he appears," Darcy began, "but in revealing his nature, I will have to expose some things that are very personal and which I would not reveal for any other reason than to see Miss Elizabeth and her sisters safe."

Mr. Gardiner's features grew grave. "He is so bad?"

Darcy nodded. "I am afraid he is."

For the next half hour, Darcy related to Elizabeth's uncle all the details of Wickham's dissipated predilections, his refusal of the living at Kympton, the squandering of his fortune, and finally, his scheme to elope with Darcy's sister.

"This is very serious indeed," Gardiner said at the end of Darcy's narration. "You think he has singled Elizabeth out to befriend because of you?"

"At the risk of sounding arrogant, I do," Darcy replied. "I do not deny he might have selected her for her beauty and wit, but I fear that I might be an added reason for his preference."

Gardiner's head bobbed up and down slowly as he thought. "I am not certain how I can help."

"Mr. Bennet seems a sensible sort of man," Darcy began. "Perhaps, a few words of caution regarding Wickham's tendency to acquire debt might set him on guard."

Gardiner shrugged. "It is worth an attempt. I shall find a way to mention it." He paused. "Might I hint that Mr. Wickham is a seducer? I would not mention your sister, of course."

Darcy nodded. "It is a general fact."

Gardiner blew out a breath. "And this is the man that has captured Elizabeth's attention?" He shook his head. "She is usually discerning."

"He is very practised. It is no fault of hers."

Gardiner shook his head. "Practiced he may be, but there is some fault on her part. She has chosen to listen. I blame my sisters for that. They are the worst gossips — always listening for some tantalizing tale to share and then imparting their stories with great embellishment. A child should not be subjected to such a demonstration from her mother." He rose from his chair. "I have cautioned Bennet about that on more than one occasion. Even the brightest will be influenced to err on occasion." He took his great coat from a hook on the wall and smiled reassuringly at Darcy. "Do not fear; Elizabeth is not like her mother. She has just forgotten her good sense in her dislike of you." He held the door open. "Not that she actually dislikes you, according to Addie."

"So, I have been told," Darcy replied.

Gardiner clapped him on the back. "Do not be discouraged. The female mind it is a delicate and complex thing. It is my belief that we gentlemen could study it all our lives and still only feign an understanding."

Darcy and Bingley added their agreement as they accompanied Mr. Gardiner out to the street.

~*~*~

A light rain was beginning to fall as Bingley reached his home after delivering Darcy to his and spending an hour or so discussing the afternoon and the changes that they hoped would soon be coming. Darcy was, understandably, more concerned for his fate than Bingley would ever be, now that he knew Jane would welcome his addresses. Bingley climbed down from the carriage and, pulling his collar close, hurried into the house.

"The Hursts are here," Jenkins said as he greeted his employer. "And Miss Clark. They are having tea in the drawing room with Miss Bingley, sir."

Bingley thanked him for the information and then stood for a moment in the corridor pondering what he should do. It would be the polite thing to greet his guests and relations, but he had very little desire to do so. His day had been rather pleasant to this point, and Caroline was guaranteed to put a damper on his mood.

"Colonel Fitzwilliam called earlier." Jenkins' voice penetrated Bingley's deliberation.

"Will he be returning?" Perhaps if he were, it could be an excuse to see Caroline for a very brief amount of time without raising her suspicion that he was put out with her — which he was.

"No, sir. He grumbled something about his mother forcing him to attend a soiree and asked if I would allow him to leave you a message. The missive is on your desk as he requested." The butler gave Bingley a significant look and lowered his voice. "He did not wish for the information to be seen by any but you."

Bingley smiled. "Very good. Then, I suppose I shall have to attend to that before I greet my sister?"

His butler shook his head. "I should think it would be better to greet your guests for a few moments before begging off to attend to duty. Your name has been bandied about a good deal."

Bingley cocked his head to the right and studied his butler. "My sisters are scheming?"

Jenkins' brows lifted and lowered, nothing else on his person or in his expression shifted, but it was enough of an answer for Bingley.

"Miss Clark?"

Again, the butler's brows gave his acknowledgment.

Bingley sighed. "Very well, I shall make my appearance and be gone as quickly as I can be. See that some tea finds its way to my study and ensure there is a bit of brandy to add to it."

Jenkins bowed and went to do as instructed.

"Blast," Bingley muttered as he straightened his sleeves and prepared to enter the drawing room. Caroline would never be satisfied until she had directed every last morsel of his life. First, she kept him from returning to Hertfordshire with suggestions that Miss Bennet did not like him — a fact which Miss Bennet had made perfectly clear was false with her admission that he should not have been persuaded away from Netherfield.

Then, Caroline had treated a friend, as she had insisted Miss Bennet was, in such a contemptible fashion. Most likely, it had been in an attempt to embitter Miss Bennet against him in case they should ever chance to meet.

As he pondered his sister's behaviour, he felt his displeasure with her growing to the point it had been last night when her perfidy had been discovered. Drawing a deep breath, he pushed the door to the room open. Caroline might think she was in control of how his future would unfold, but she was not. And, if she were not careful, she would also not be in control of her own destiny, for he would make certain she was well-settled in some gentleman's home as quickly as could be, just as Mr. Gardiner had suggested.

"Charles!" Caroline cried in delight as he entered. "We had begun to despair of seeing you at all."

Bingley placed a kiss on the hand she held out to him and then greeted Louisa and Hurst before waiting to be introduced to Caroline's friend, who had begun fidgeting with her skirt and moistened her lips when he entered.

"Have you met Miss Clark?" Caroline asked. "We spend at least a portion of every soiree in each other's company, but I cannot remember if you have been properly introduced."

Bingley narrowed his eyes and scrutinised his sister's friend with a slight scowl on his lips. It was rude perhaps, but the lady was wearing a very cat-like expression and looking at him as if he were a bowl of cream. "No, I do not believe we have been introduced. Welcome," he finally said. There were several other things that he wished to say, but he clamped his mouth shut and kept his speculations about her standing and wealth to himself. He knew his sister did not befriend anyone who was anything less than a gentleman's daughter with a sizable fortune. He cursed himself silently. Such a fact should have alerted him to his sister's insincerity toward Miss Bennet. For though Jane was a gentleman's daughter, she was not wealthy and held no sway in the ton.

"Miss Clark is attending the Johnson's musicale tonight just as we are," Caroline continued.

"The Johnson's musicale?" Bingley repeated. "Are you attending with Hurst and Louisa?"

"And you." Caroline laughed lightly.

Bingley shook his head. "I do not remember accepting any invitation."

"Oh, but you did. Last week. I asked if I could attend, and you thought it would be an excellent thing." Caroline explained.

Bingley shifted from one foot to another. "And I suppose it is, as long as you go with Hurst and not me."

"But I accepted for both of us. Mrs. Johnson and

Marietta will be exceedingly disappointed if you do not attend."

Bingley shrugged. Marietta Johnson was another of Caroline's friends whom his sister kept mentioning on a regular basis. Apparently, her father's estate was old enough, and Miss Johnson's dowry was large enough for him to consider her as a possible wife. "Tell them I have a sore throat or a headache or some such thing."

Caroline gasped.

"I have been out all day and have business that requires my attention and am in no mood to sit about and listen to song after song." He turned to Hurst. "You are escorting Louisa to this musicale, are you not?"

Hurst shrugged and nodded. "It seems I am."

"There you are, Caroline. You may go and see and be seen as you wish, and I can have a quiet night with my ledgers."

Caroline had crossed her arms and was pouting while Miss Clark was looking curiously between the two of them.

Bingley grimaced. He had gone too far in being disagreeable it seemed.

"I say, you have become a right stodgy old bore," Caroline grumbled.

"Yes, well, the delights of town do not enthrall me as much as you, and you know my dislike of sitting for hours."

"Yet you will sit behind your desk all night?"

He shook his head. "No, I shall pace a fair bit between bouts of sitting."

"My brother does not favour being idle either," Miss Clark interjected. "He often stands along the wall when he attends musicales with me. You could stand with him."

"An excellent idea!" Caroline cried.

Yes, Bingley thought to himself, that would set a few tongues to wagging if Miss Clark were to attend a soiree with Caroline while he stood along the wall and conversed with the lady's brother. Every interested wag would have them at the church's door before the fourth piece of music had ended.

"And who will tend to my business whilst I stand about looking foolish?"

"You will not look foolish," Caroline said with a laugh. "You will be amiable and charming as you always are. You will not lack for entertainment."

"I do not wish for entertainment."

"Please?" Caroline begged. "You have not attended a soiree in over a week. People are beginning to talk."

Bingley tipped his head. "About what?"

Caroline bit her lip and ducked her head as she stole a secret look at her friend. "That you have been jilted and are wallowing in heartbreak."

Bingley crossed his arms. "And my being seen at a function with one of your friends on my arm will put these rumors to rest?" His tone did not disguise his disbelief.

"Of course." Caroline blinked wide eyes at him. "You must be seen in the company of someone if you wish for the rumors to stop."

"Precisely why should I care about these rumors?"

"A man who has been jilted for who knows what reason the gossips create will find it hard to secure a good match."

Bingley chuckled. "Not if he has my fortune. Now, if you will excuse me, I have business that needs my attention." He turned and hurried to his study.

The tea he had requested and a small glass of

brandy were on his desk. He eased himself into his chair and pulled the missive addressed to him out from under the corner of the tea tray.

B-

Letter sent. Should have a response within the week.

Mother insists I attend the Johnson's musicale tonight. Your sister said you were attending. Johnson's library is good for escaping the ordeal. Curious to hear about your mission. Bring Darcy.

R-

Bingley sighed, took out his pen, and scratched a note to Darcy on the paper below Richard's message. Then, after folding, addressing, and sealing it, he rang for Jenkins to have it delivered.

He shook his head as he stood in front of his desk and poured a healthy dose of the brandy into his tea before finishing what remained in the glass. Caroline would be far too pleased to have him capitulate to her demands so soon after having refused. He rounded his desk and sank into his chair once again. There was no need to tell her until dinner. He would savour this cup of tea, push around a few books, and consider his happy future until then.

Chapter 7

Bingley stood near the door in the Johnson's music room. He had seen his sister to her seat and then left both her and her friend in Hurst's care. Caroline had, of course, protested in her teasing, cajoling fashion. However, he had reminded her that Miss Clark suggested that he stand, and she had agreed that her friend's idea was an excellent one.

He smiled even now, as he found a piece of wall to lean against, at how her jaw had clenched in displeasure as she attempted to remain pleasing should anyone hear their conversation. He was certain she and Miss Clark were equally as displeased that he had not gone to stand with Mr. Clark. In fact, Bingley had made certain to stand on the side of the room opposite of that gentleman. Wagging tongues would always wag, but it was not his intent to give them something about which to whisper.

He pulled his watch from his pocket and glanced at it. The music should begin soon. From where he was standing, he could just catch a glimpse of the entry. It seemed as if they were in for a crush this evening. Indeed, every gentleman not already lining the walls would soon be in deference to his lady's being allowed a place to sit. Such a sizable crowd would also make it much easier to slip out of the throng and hideaway.

Ah, there was Richard.

Lady Matlock was whispering something to him. He nodded and then followed behind his parents, stopping when they did to greet the few people who had not yet entered the music room.

"Pardon me," a footman said as he slipped in front of Bingley on his way to help another open the doors that joined this room to the drawing room beyond. Unsurprisingly, the drawing room had been rearranged so that its furniture and, Bingley imagined, a few extra pieces from the other room were facing the instruments positioned in the alcove created by the large bow window on the front of the house.

Mrs. Johnson was a seasoned hostess. She had kept the room small until the numbers had begun to look impressive. Only then, had she thrown open the doors to the room she knew she would need to add. It was a bit of staging — a few dramatics that lent themselves to how successful her soiree had been. After all, the room was not large enough to hold the attendees. Almost inevitably, tomorrow, there would be someone in all the most important drawing rooms in town commenting on her success.

Bingley shook his head and chuckled. Some of these society matrons would make shrewd businesswomen. Presenting things to best effect, scheming to arrange meetings, wrangling willing daughters and less-than-willing gentlemen into life-long contracts — yes, they would likely own all of England and a half or better of the West Indies in a very small space of time should they put their minds to such a task. And heaven help the poor fellow who attempted to stand in their way! Even Prinny would find it difficult to contain such a movement.

A shoulder pumped against Bingley's, drawing his attention away from the way Mrs. Johnson was fluttering about with her daughter close behind her.

"Where is Darcy?" Richard asked.

"I assume he will be here in," Bingley drew his watch out once again, "two minutes as the music is to begin in five."

Richard chuckled.

Both men knew that Darcy did not like to be tardy to any engagement, but he also did not like to arrive early since arriving early meant he would be expected to stand around and converse politely about trivial matters.

As if the mention of his name had conjured him, Bingley caught a glimpse of his friend at the entrance. "He's early," Bingley said, nodding his head toward the door. "What were your mother's instructions?" Bingley snapped his watch closed and tucked it into his pocket. "I saw her speaking to you in the hall."

"I am not to sneak out to the garden, and I am to be civil to at least three ladies this evening." Richard smirked. "I have already spoken to three ladies so that requirement is met. As for the garden, I have no intention of strolling about the garden with its dimly lit areas where a compromise could be affected when we could retire to the safer confines of the library."

"You think there are ladies here who would try to trap you into marriage?" Bingley asked with a chuckle.

Richard shrugged. "It would not be the first attempt. There are those who wish for a connection to my father, but I have no desire to sacrifice myself just to elevate some lady to daughter-in-law of the Earl of Matlock."

"Unless, of course," Bingley added with a smirk, "she has a fortune that is as handsome as she is."

Richard nodded. "Precisely. I shall throw myself on no matrimonial swords unless the conditions are in my favour. Darcy," he greeted as his cousin joined him. "Quite a crush, is it not?"

"My favourite sort of event," Darcy replied grimly.

"Two songs," Richard whispered. "My mother will stop looking back here after that, and then we can make our escape."

"Am I going to run afoul of your mother?" Darcy asked.

"Most likely," Richard replied with a grin. "Consider it practice for when you make your intentions known regarding a certain young lady."

Darcy shook his head. Teasing words seemed to

roll off his cousin's tongue as easily as butter slid from a heated knife. There was seldom a time when Richard found himself without a witty rejoinder. It was something Darcy had always envied, for, to him, ease in conversation only came when he was with a small group of intimate acquaintances. A room filled to overflowing, as this one was, made him uneasy and often muddled his thoughts.

His father had stressed to him the need to never bring shame to the Darcy name. With that in mind, every word needed to be measured carefully before being spoken.

Darcy shifted, moving his weight from his right foot to his left, as their hostess welcomed the assembled masses and introduced her daughter, who was to begin the evening with a piece performed on the violin.

Perhaps if he had considered his words more carefully in Meryton, he would not now find himself loving a lady who had very little liking for him.

For the duration of two songs, he pondered his various meetings with Miss Elizabeth. Then, when the third song began, he followed his cousin and Bingley out of the room and down the hall to the library.

The library was not wholly unoccupied. Mr. Johnson gave the young gentlemen a smile and a nod as they entered.

"Your mother will be displeased if you spend the whole of your time in here," he said to Richard.

Richard allowed it to be so but assured the gentleman that they were only attempting to find a quiet spot to have a bit of a tête-à-tête and would not be overly long.

Mr. Johnson chuckled as if he knew very well that the three men would be in his library as long as they thought they could stay. "I have a daughter," he said. "This room could be yours at every function my wife holds."

"It nearly always is now," Richard returned with a grin. "The desk is a very nice addition."

Mr. Johnson shook his head. "Fitzwilliam, why do you attend if you are only going to hie off to the library."

"My mother," Richard replied as he took a seat in a group of chairs as far removed from the door as the room would allow.

"I know my Marietta is not the incomparable of the season, but she is not without her charms," he tried again.

"She is lovely," Richard said.

"And well dowered," Mr. Johnson interjected.

"Indeed," Richard agreed. "However, these two have their hearts set elsewhere, and I, no matter what my mother might say, am bound to my commission and, as such, am not at present looking for a wife."

"Very well," Mr. Johnson replied with a smile. "I should like to know more about the ladies that have turned your friends' heads, but I will refrain. Unless..."

Richard chuckled. "We are not at liberty at this time to divulge any particulars, sir. The campaign has only begun, and we dare not rouse too many suspicions before the plan of attack is set in motion."

"Very well, men, carry on." Mr. Johnson gave a jaunty salute and returned his attention to his book. "I am only allowed to remain here until the intermission," he added, "and I will direct your mother here if she inquires after you, Fitzwilliam."

"Understood, and thank you, sir," Richard replied. He and Mr. Johnson had held many discussions in this room during soirees. Mr. Johnson was a reasonable man, and if his daughter were not so much like her mother and more like her father, Richard might have considered her just to gain a man like Mr. Johnson as a father-in-law. They got on quite well together.

"Your mission was successful?" Richard asked as he turned his attention to Bingley and Darcy.

Bingley smiled broadly. "Extremely. I have both Miss Bennet's and her uncle's permission to continue calling on her."

"Excellent! And Darcy?"

"Mrs. Gardiner is going to attempt to persuade Miss Elizabeth to come for a visit," Darcy replied.

"So, until then, we wait on that front," Richard muttered.

Darcy nodded.

"Tell me about the aunt and uncle," Richard said, settling back in his chair and preparing to listen to a full account of everything Bingley and Darcy had observed, and he was not to be disappointed. Bingley spoke highly of everything, as Richard knew he would. Bingley was easily pleased when there was no reason not to be, and from everything that his cousin added, there appeared to be nothing that would be displeasing.

"And you told him the whole story regarding Wickham?" Richard asked in surprise.

Darcy nodded. "He can be trusted."

"You are certain?" Richard questioned.

"Yes."

There was no moment of pause, no falter in tone that spoke of any unease on Darcy's part. "Very well," Richard replied, "Then, I will trust your judgment."

"Come meet him," Darcy offered. "I know you will agree." He smirked. "It would be good to have you on my side when I have to defend a tradesman to your father."

Richard chuckled. "You'll have little trouble with Father. Aunt Catherine, on the other hand..." He paused and raised his hand in acknowledgment of Mr. Johnson's leaving. "We will have to prepare ourselves for her, eventually, when you are finally successful, that is."

Darcy knew it was true. "As soon as I am successful, I will write to her and inform her of how things stand."

"And you expect her to just accept your words?"

No, Darcy did not expect anything of the kind. He expected a vocal protest either by post or in person. Lady Catherine was never one to be put off easily about the smallest thing, and the refusal to marry her daughter and to marry, instead, a lady with an uncle in trade would be tantamount to a call to arms for Lady Catherine.

"Perhaps," Bingley suggested, "you could be married before you wrote to her."

This caused both Darcy and Richard to chuckle and admit that such a plan might indeed be best. A few suggestions — both practical ones and fanciful ones — as to how it might be accomplished were then passed around the group for a time until the library door opened slightly and the three fell silent.

"Your mother?" Darcy whispered to Richard as he could clearly hear that the voice filtering in from the hall was that of a lady.

"Perhaps," Richard returned but then shook his head as he heard giggling. "Mother rarely giggles," he whispered.

"They are either in here, or the garden," a distinctly familiar voice said from outside the half-opened door.

Bingley groaned. "It is worse than your mother. That is Caroline." He rose. "It would be best if we were all in a more populated area if we are to be accosted by her and her friend."

Richard's brows rose. "You do not trust them?"

"If you had seen the way Miss Clark licked her lips and nearly purred in my drawing room when I entered today, you would not trust them either. My sister is scheming."

Darcy and Richard joined Bingley in crossing the room to the door.

"Just stumble on the carpet or catch your toe on the heel of your other slipper. He will not let you fall, and then, when you are in his arms, I will make sure that someone sees it or hears about it."

Bingley stood with the doorknob within arm's length of him and could clearly hear his sister's instructions. He motioned for Richard to open the door. "Open it quickly. Just do not catch her if she falls," he hissed.

And fall Caroline did. Right at her brother's feet and with a rather loud plop when Richard yanked the door open.

"Caroline!" Bingley cried in surprise, extending a hand to help her to her feet. "How many times have you been told not to be listening at doors?"

Caroline allowed him to help her from the floor.

Her cheeks burned a brilliant red. "I was not listening at the door. I was looking for you."

"At least, you are somewhat honest. However, you have left out the part that you were scheming. You should know that if Miss Clark or any of your other friends flings herself at me, I will allow them to fall just as you did, and I will not marry her, no matter what it does to either her reputation or mine. I will not be trapped, Caroline." He gave a small bow and began to move around his fuming sister and her stunned friend.

"You must forget her," Caroline whispered as her brother brushed past her.

Bingley stopped mid-stride. "I shall only forget her when my heart stops beating."

"Charles, do be reasonable. She was a pretty plaything. Someone to pass the time. She is not who you need. You will soon come to know I am right." Caroline shrugged under her brother's glare as if not affected by it in the least. "And I am certain I can find the perfect lady for you."

"No," Bingley snapped. "You will not find any lady for me. You will not even suggest any lady to me. If I have not found that for what I wish within a month's time, I am returning to Netherfield and attempting to persuade the lady who holds my heart to have me."

"You cannot," Caroline cried, her eyes darting to Darcy.

Darcy shrugged. "He seems determined," he said nonchalantly. He knew it was not the reply Caroline expected. She likely expected him to support her in her claims that Miss Bennet was not a wise choice. However, having come to understand what it was to have one's heart completely engaged by a lady and to not wish for any other, Darcy would not support any scheme of hers to interfere between Bingley and Miss Bennet. In fact, he would do all he could to ensure that nothing came between them.

Caroline gasped. "I will not allow it!"

"You cannot stop me," Bingley growled.

"I believe I can," Caroline replied with a flick of her head.

"Hurst will see you home. We are through. Darcy, if you do not mind, I should very much appreciate a ride home."

"Certainly. Richard, if you wish to join us, you may."

Richard nodded. "As soon as I find my mother and tell her I am leaving."

"I will wait ten minutes," Darcy said before turning to hurry after Bingley.

Richard waved his acceptance, then turned to Caroline and Miss Clark. "Ladies, I do hope your evening improves," he said with a bow as he took his leave.

Chapter 8

Bingley made certain not to be available when his sister arrived home later that night, and in the morning, he took his breakfast in his study with strict orders to Jenkins that he was not to be disturbed by his sister. Then, after a few moments of clearing up some accounts and writing instructions to a particular milliner that credit was not to be extended to his sister beyond a certain point, he went in search of her.

He found her at the piano forte, attempting to master a new piece of music.

Standing at the door, he listened for a moment or two before entering. She was not a proficient, but she was every bit as good as the two ladies he had heard last night at the Johnsons' home. Caroline was not without accomplishments, nor was she lacking in beauty. What his sister lacked was sense enough to realize that her ambitions were not to be fulfilled. Even if Miss Elizabeth refused the position, Caroline would never be the mistress of Pemberley. Darcy was not inclined to tie himself to a lady like Caroline for the simple fact that Caroline was grasping, and she lacked the sort of wit that would challenge Darcy. In fact, Bingley was quite certain that Caroline would never dispute with Darcy on much, and no matter how much Darcy liked to be right and in charge of every detail, Bingley knew that his friend craved stimulating conversation and having his opinions questioned — at least, at times. He chuckled to himself. There were moments when challenging an opinion would rile Darcy into a fit of temper. Richard was proficient at marching directly up to that point of breaking and then, with a laugh and a tease, retreating to a safer position. Bingley had witnessed it on several occasions.

At the instrument, Caroline moved the new piece of music to the side and pulled out another.

"I am off. Do not hold dinner for me, for I do not know when I will return," he said as he crossed to where his sister sat. "I have had the knocker removed from the door and have given instructions that it not be returned until I return or Louisa arrives to be a chaperone for any callers."

"Where are you going?" Caroline asked in surprise.

"Anywhere that is not here," Bingley replied with a small shrug. "I find I do not wish for your company at present."

"Charles," Caroline's voice was soothing, "surely you cannot be angry with me for wishing to see you well-matched."

Bingley's smile was tight as he willed himself to remain calm. He knew that the disagreement they had broached last night in the Johnsons' library needed to be revisited and that he needed to make his position regarding whom he married clear, but he had hoped to delay it a bit longer. However, knowing what the note in his hand said, a delay was not actually feasible but merely a wish that was not destined to be granted.

"I am certain I should not be put out in the least if you showed even one ounce of concern about whether I was happy with such a match," he said, taking up the argument of his happiness and wielding it in front of his sister.

"But I do wish for you to be happy," she parried.

"Happy and well-matched. If we are to rise above our beginnings and pass that new standing on to our children, we must align ourselves to best advantage." She smoothed the pages of her next musical selection on the top of the instrument. "Do you not wish for your son to be more readily accepted in society than either of us were?"

There had been and still were, at times, sticking points when mixing with some in society. It was why Bingley was actively pursuing the purchase of land. For with the purchase of an estate with its fields and tenants came entrance to that group on the edge of which he could now only circulate because of his wealth and connection to Darcy but to which he could not become a member.

Land. Land was needed to become what his father had wished him to be — a gentleman in every sense of the word — educated, noble in character, and an owner of land. He knew, however, that even with his purchase of an estate, there would still be those who would think him inferior simply because his father had been a tradesman. That would not change. Though he were to marry the daughter of a king, there would still be those who would remind him of his heritage, for such is the way of some people, people who were only able to feel superior when making others appear and feel less important.

"We cannot erase who our father was," he said to his sister. "And I do not wish to remove his memory from our family. My children will know of their grandfather. He was a great man and an excellent father, Caroline." His words must have struck a chord with her, for she turned her head away, but not before he saw the glint of tears in her eyes.

"He was a tradesman," she whispered.

"Yes, he was, and he always will be. However, he has provided well enough for me to purchase my standing as a gentleman and for you to have a generous dowry that will make it easier for you to marry a gentleman, thereby, raising your standing." He placed the note he held in his hand on the piano. "I would not be lowering myself by marrying a gentleman's daughter such as Miss Bennet. You know this."

"But her uncles are not gentlemen." Caroline lifted her chin, unwilling to admit that he was correct.

Bingley shook his head. Caroline was stubborn, foolishly stubborn. She had been all her life, and he knew that reasoning with her when her mind was set on something was nigh onto impossible. He tapped the note he had placed on the instrument. "Last night you attempted to arrange a compromise and force me into a marriage not of my choosing. This is a copy of a message that has been sent. It is the first of many which I will write limiting your spending at all your favourite shops. Should I even catch a whisper of you scheming in such a fashion again, another merchant will be made aware of your lack of funds."

Caroline's eyes grew wide as she read the missive her brother had written. "But there will be talk of us being poor."

"Perhaps," Bingley replied, "but that is your choice. Act wisely, and you shall retain your privilege to shop as you wish. Behave as you did last night and prepare to be the object of gossip and disdain."

Her eyes narrowed, her cheeks grew red, and she set her jaw firmly.

"I will marry as I choose."

"You will ruin us both," she hissed.

"Have you so little faith in me?"

"You would marry ..." She waved her hand

toward the window in a circular motion as she sought for the right word. "A country miss of no standing. No! Less than no standing," she rose from the stool on which she sat. "Jane Bennet is a nobody, Charles, a nobody with an uncle in trade!" She paced to the window and back, her anger evident in the measured and heavy steps she took. "I suppose you would have Darcy marry her sister as well. I saw how she flirted with him. Pretending not to like him and drawing him along. Why! That is just what Jane did with you. Batting her eyes and smiling demurely! They are fortune hunters, Charles. Nothing more than fortune hunters, trained by their mother to snare the wealthiest man that enters the neighbourhood!"

"Darcy will also marry whom he chooses, and it will not be you." Bingley kept his voice calm, not because he knew it would do little good to raise it, but because he knew that keeping his voice placid would provoke his sister much more effectively. And after hearing such statements about Jane and Elizabeth as his sister had just spewed, he found he wished to provoke her.

"He would marry me if you would promote me to him," Caroline snapped.

"Darcy would not marry you if I offered him twice your dowry." He captured her wrist just before her hand made contact with his face. "You are a tradesman's daughter, but that is not what keeps him from offering for you. You have not caught his interest. You are not what he seeks, and it is time you look for a match elsewhere."

"Pemberley will be mine," she sputtered.

Bingley held her wrist a moment longer. "I will not force him to do his duty to you no matter what position you might arrange for him to be discovered in with you. I would send you to our aunt and refuse to sign any papers or allow for a marriage. Do I make myself clear?" He released her hand only after she had given a small nod of her head.

"It might be best," he continued as he moved toward the door, "if you were to remove to Louisa's home. I will call on Hurst and see if he is amenable. I do not trust you and your friends not to arrange some folly that will end in some poor lady's ruin and retreat from society along with yours."

He closed the door firmly behind him. He had no desire to stay and listen to her protests, and he knew there would be many. Caroline liked Louisa, but Hurst was not her favourite person with whom to spend time. But then, again, she did not like spending time with anyone who did not always agree with her, and Hurst did not always agree with anyone. His opinion often shifted with his mood, and his ability to recall what he had said before was inversely proportional to the amount of port that had accompanied a discussion. Caroline found it all very annoying. She had complained of it often enough to her brother, but only once to their sister.

Louisa, though having only married for the sake of a good match, had found she did not despise her husband or his odd ways. In fact, on the one occasion when Caroline had complained about Hurst to her, Louisa had made it clear that she not only respected her husband due to his position, but she also found his eccentricities to be endearing. Bingley smiled at the thought of his sister stumbling upon love in a relationship that she had entered as a marriage of convenience.

His horse was waiting for him when he exited the house, and with only one glance at the window to the music room and a small ache in his heart for the rift that had grown between him and his sister, he rode off to call first on Hurst and then to meet Darcy before calling at the Gardiners.

His plans, however, were to be upset in a most pleasant fashion, for when he arrived at Darcy House, he found Mrs. Gardiner and Miss Bennet in the sitting room, conversing with Darcy's sister, Georgiana, as well as Georgiana's companion, Mrs. Annesley, and Richard while Darcy attempted now and again to add to the discourse.

Darcy pulled out his watch and looked at it and then Bingley as Bingley was announced. The others in the room might not have seen the slight rise of Darcy's brow, but Bingley did not miss it. It was the same expression with which Bingley was always greeted when he was late for a meeting with Darcy. Arriving just on time for a social gathering was acceptable as was being several minutes early for a meeting; however, tardiness was always met with disapprobation.

"I have a very good reason for being late," Bingley said to Darcy after he had made all the proper greetings. "However, I had expected to be on our way to Gracechurch Street rather than here." He smiled broadly. "Not that I am disappointed."

"We were just about to leave for a shopping

excursion when Mr. Darcy's note arrived inviting us to call on him here today," Mrs. Gardiner explained, her lips puckering into a small smirk before continuing. "I believe he wished for his sister and cousin to meet me. I did attempt to lure my husband away from his work, but he was unable to be tempted, even for such a treat as this." She waved her hand indicating the room and its occupants.

Darcy chuckled. "I admit it was so my sister and cousin could meet both Miss Bennet and Mrs. Gardiner."

Mrs. Gardiner raised a teasing brow. "Do we pass? Are we acceptable despite our address?"

Richard guffawed. "You are refreshing, Mrs. Gardiner. I do not think I have met another who is so direct in broaching a subject. I quite like it."

Mrs. Gardiner's eyes grew wide. "Oh, I assure you that I am not always so direct. I do know how to be demure. However, with friends — and I do hope we are friends — I find it much better to avoid any sort of equivocation."

"We are friends," Darcy assured her. "And I believe from my cousin's response, you have gained his approval."

Mrs. Gardiner gave a small nod of her head in acceptance and then looked at Miss Darcy and Mrs. Annesley. "I do hope I have not been a poor example."

Mrs. Annesley shook her head. "I have found your manners to be noteworthy, and my charge knows there is a difference between how we act in our homes with our closest friends and family and how we comport ourselves when in a public setting. However, it is good to hear you reiterate what I have taught."

"I find no fault in you," Georgiana said with a smile.

"But it remains a fact that some will, no matter my manners or words or dress. I am a tradesman's wife. He is an honorable man of substantial wealth, but," she held up a finger, "he is not a gentleman. He owns no land, nor does he desire to own any. He is very happy with his life and position. If he were to remove from town for longer than a month or two, he would grow restless and become bored. He was made for making deals and seeing things done. Oh, I know a landowner must possess such skills as well, but he would miss the excitement of seeing a new shipment arrive full of possibilities and promise of gain."

"My father was the same," Bingley said. "He enjoyed so much of what he did. It was not a trial for him to throw himself into his work." He shook his head. "What would tire me just at the thought would invigorate him. That is why he did not seek to purchase land but left it to me to do. I do not have his motivation for such things. I find I would prefer the responsibilities of a landowner."

"Just like our John," Mrs. Gardiner said with a smile. "He will be the one to move his father's fortune from a warehouse and stores to an estate."

"I should like to meet your son sometime," said Bingley.

"As long as there are biscuits?" Mrs. Gardiner asked.

Bingley shrugged. "Perhaps even if there are not."

Mrs. Gardiner laughed. "My husband would scold me for controlling the conversation." She looked directly at Georgiana. "It is a fault with which I struggle."

"I have enjoyed listening to you," Georgiana

admitted. "I have felt quite at ease." She darted a look at her brother. "I do not always feel so."

"You are like your brother," Mrs. Gardiner whispered.

Georgiana returned the woman's smile and nodded.

"I should like to hear Bingley's reason for being late," said Richard.

"Caroline," Bingley replied and, with a small huff of frustration, shook his head. "I stopped at Hurst's to inquire about her removing to his house for a time."

Darcy's were not the only brows that rose at the statement. In fact, there was not a brow that remained unaffected by such a declaration.

"I do not trust her after last night." He blew out a breath. "She attempted to find a way to compromise me with one of her friends — a lady she claims would be a good match," he explained to those who had not been in the Johnsons' library. "We had a discussion about it before I left today that did not sit well with her." He held Darcy's gaze. "She claims that Pemberley will be hers, and I have told her that I would never allow it."

When Bingley had finished speaking, silence reigned for several minutes.

"I had hoped to discuss something that I have been pondering since your call yesterday." Jane's cheeks flushed, and her eyes lowered for a moment before rising once again, filled with determination.

"Please continue," Darcy encouraged before Bingley could.

Jane gave him a grateful smile. "When we last spoke, we considered the fact that your aunt will not be pleased if you are successful in winning my sister's heart."

Bingley watched Georgiana's face as Jane spoke to Darcy. From the lack of surprise, he surmised that Georgiana had been told of Darcy's intentions to marry.

"And we must still consider that," Jane continued. "However, I have been considering how best to..." Her brows furrowed, and her lips pursed as she considered her words. She took a breath and smoothed her expression. "How best to prevent Miss Bingley from interfering with either your plan to marry," her lips curled into a smile and her eyes sparkled, "or mine," she concluded.

"You are determined to marry?" Delight filled Bingley as he asked it.

Jane lifted her chin and met his gaze. "I am," she replied simply. "However, I should not like to have to share a home with a woman who has caused me pain and treated me poorly."

Darcy watched Jane with pleased surprise. The Jane he had met yesterday, who was more forward and less reserved than the one he had met in Hertfordshire, seemed not to have been a figment of a moment but of an enduring nature.

"I can send her to live with our aunt. I do not see Hurst abiding her presence for more than a few months," Bingley replied.

"That would be effective as long as your aunt remains well, but what if the worst should befall her? Then where would your sister reside?"

Bingley blew out a breath and shrugged. "I would hope she might be married," he said uncertainly. Knowing how abominably she had treated Jane, he had no desire to have his sister in his house after he married, for he could see her causing trouble just to prove that she had been correct about Jane not being the best choice of wife.

Jane smoothed her skirt, her eyes watching her

hands' motions. "Why hope?" she asked, lifting her eyes to his again.

Bingley could see the unease that mingled with determination in her features, and he admired her courage as he waited for her to continue.

She swallowed and drew a fortifying breath. "It could be arranged."

Chapter 9

"Arranged?" Bingley repeated the word with no small amount of surprise. Was Jane suggesting that they arrange to compromise Caroline? He had not thought his Jane could be so scheming. While it was shocking, it was not off-putting. In fact, if he were candid about the feelings it stirred within him, it was rather appealing that she would go to such lengths to have a happy future with him and to provide the same for her sister and Darcy.

"I know it is not proper," Jane said quickly, her courage faltering at the startled look on Bingley's face. "But your sister has not treated either you or me well, and I dare say she has not spoken favourably about my sister to Mr. Darcy. If she were to know that we were arranging things so that a match might occur between my sister and your friend, I am certain she would find some way to interfere just as she has between us." As she spoke her anger at how she had been duped into believing Caroline was a friend when in actuality she was nothing more than someone at whom Caroline might laugh rose. She clasped her hands in her lap and squared her shoulders. She would not faint now. She would continue on.

"In fact, I believe the reason she interfered at all between you and me can be set solely on the fact that Mr. Darcy showed interest in Elizabeth. If you were to remain at Netherfield, so would Mr. Darcy. That simply could not be allowed if your sister was to win the prize of Pemberley, which you have just now claimed is her continued goal. Therefore, one and all must be removed from Netherfield and such a danger. And one must not encourage any connection with someone like myself here in town. Why what would happen if you and I should decide to marry, and you would return to Netherfield before she could effectively ensnare her prize? Would Mr. Darcy return to Netherfield with you for a time? Would he be a guest at our home? Would he continue to be enamored with my sister? It really would be far too dangerous to allow any of that."

"She has a point," said Richard. "A very good point." He smiled. "You are just as delightful as your aunt. Are all the members of your family so astute?"

Jane felt her cheeks begin to burn at such a compliment as she laughed lightly. "No, I fear they are not. Elizabeth is to be sure, Mama has her moments, and my father can outshine us all when he is roused to it. However, my younger sisters seem to lack depth. Mary shows potential if she would but see things in degrees rather than absolutes. However, Kitty and Lydia show no desire to think beyond what appears before them unless they are scheming to get their way."

Richard chuckled. "Then I would have to disagree with you, for it sounds like all your sisters could be counted among the great minds of England in some fashion if they were directed properly."

"That is it precisely," said Mrs. Gardiner. "There is much potential in them all. However, there is a sad lack of guidance, and that is all I will say on that subject." She gave a sharp nod of her head to punctuate her determination to speak no further.

"Do you have a plan for how we might deal with

Miss Bingley?" Richard could not hide his interest in such as scheme — not that his interest in a scheme came as a surprise to any who knew him.

Jane raised a shoulder and let it fall. "Are there any gentlemen who might catch her eye, and who might be encouraged to pay particular attention to her with the goal of engaging her affections?"

"None that own Pemberley," Darcy muttered.

"She is so fixed?" Jane asked.

Bingley nodded. "Napoleon would more readily give up France to England than my sister will give up pursuing what she wants. She is a very determined sort of person. She always has been." Bingley could not hide the frustration and anger he felt toward his sister.

"It is a good trait if it can be properly directed." Mrs. Gardiner's voice was soothing.

"Indeed, it is," Mrs. Annesley agreed.

Bingley could not help but smile at how both women were attempting to ease his mind. "I am certain it will someday serve her well."

"There is Sir Matthew Broadhurst," Georgiana said quietly. "He has just arrived in town, and from what I have heard, he is rather attractive — broad shoulders, fine legs, wavy brown hair, deep brown eyes, and a pleasant expression. He is also said to be wealthy and heir to a lovely estate in Surrey. And," Georgiana's brows raised to add emphasis as she continued, "he has a title. There is little to dislike about such credentials."

"It does not hurt our cause," Mrs. Annesley added, "that his uncle's will requires him to marry before he can take possession of his inheritance beyond the title. Therefore, he is actively seeking a bride this season."

Jane's brows furrowed. "If he is all those things, why is he still unattached?"

Georgiana grimaced. "Mrs. Allard says he seems rather quiet and reserved."

"Would he be ill-used by a lady who is neither of those things?" Jane asked in all seriousness. She wished to see Caroline married, and married well, but she did not wish to injure an unsuspecting gentleman in the process.

"Oh, no," Georgiana replied. "Mrs. Allard said he is very fixed and unyielding in his opinions and standards. She suspects that is why he has not found success with the few ladies he has attempted to court in the past."

Jane sighed. "I do not wish to see Miss Bingley tied to an ogre even if he is titled and handsome."

"Not even if she deserves it?" Bingley asked.

"No, not even then." Jane could not be the cause of someone else's misery, even if that someone had caused a great deal of sorrow for her. She would forever feel the weight of such actions.

"There is only one way to decide," said Darcy. "We must meet him. I am certain that, between Bingley and me, we can determine if it will be an amicable match."

"You are not going to discourage us?" Bingley's mouth tipped up in a crooked half smirk.

Darcy shook his head. "I am a bit surprised that my sister is the source of knowledge on such a thing, but I find I cannot fault a plan that will see you happy and clear a portion of the path for me to claim my own happiness." He shrugged and then shook his head. "I startle myself, to be honest, but whatever part I need to play to see this through to the end, I am willing to play it."

So it was settled that, as soon as it was convenient, Bingley and Darcy would find a way to meet Sir Matthew Broadhurst and evaluate his suitability as a husband for Caroline.

It took only two days from the time the decision was made in Darcy's drawing room for an opportunity for such a meeting to occur.

As the sun was beginning its journey to its height, warming the earth and the people who had ventured out into the crisp air of a clear winter's morning, Darcy and Bingley came upon a solitary rider loping his way through the park with a groom trailing at a good distance behind him. Bingley, as he always did, tipped his hat and wished the gentleman a good morning.

The gentleman returned the gesture and then slowed his horse as he drew nearer Bingley and Darcy.

"I do not believe I have had the pleasure of making your acquaintance," he began. "I am Sir Matthew Broadhurst of Stoningham in Surrey."

"Charles Bingley," Bingley returned, "and my friend, Fitzwilliam Darcy of Pemberley in Derbyshire. It is a pleasure to meet you."

"Indeed, it is," Darcy agreed.

"I have not been to many soirees yet, and it seems I like to rise earlier than most. I believe, you gentlemen make six whom I have met since arriving in town. May I join you?" Sir Matthew drew his horse alongside them after Bingley had assured him that they would be delighted to have his company.

The gentleman appeared to be everything that Georgiana had said he was. His dress was impeccable. He appeared to be of an acceptable stature, neither too tall nor too short. He was handsome with a very pleasant and amiable, if quiet, air about him.

"I have heard that you have just recently come into your title," said Darcy. "My condolences on the loss of your uncle."

Sir Matthew's gave his thanks softly and somberly. "He was not the friendliest of men at times, and he could be demanding. However, my uncle was a good man who took my mother, my siblings, and myself into his home after my father died." He glanced over at the men beside him. "My father was the rector of the parish near Stoningham."

"Do you have many siblings?" Bingley asked.

"A younger brother and two older sisters," Sir Matthew replied. "My sisters are both married and happily settled, and my brother is studying to take orders. He is much like my father. And you, do you gentlemen have siblings?"

"I have a younger sister who has been left in my care," Darcy answered. "She is just sixteen."

"Both of your parents are gone?" Sir Matthew's voice was once again soft and soothing as he inquired.

"For several years now," Darcy answered. "It is something Bingley and I have in common."

"You do not have a parent remaining either?" Sir Matthew asked, turning to Bingley.

"No," Bingley replied. "My father died three years ago, leaving me a fortune and the care of my sisters. Louisa has married, but Caroline has not." He noted how Sir Matthew's expression spoke of the gentleman's interest in that last fact. "My father was a tradesman."

Sir Matthew's brows rose. "You do not own an estate?"

There was no censure in his tone. He seemed genuinely interested.

"Not yet," Bingley replied. "I have let an estate in Hertfordshire and am looking to purchase one in the near future."

"I wish you well in your endeavour."

There was again a genuineness to the man's words that impressed both Bingley and Darcy.

"I cannot claim my estate until I marry." Sir Matthew shook his head. "My uncle knew that if he did not force me out of the house and to seriously consider taking a wife, I would bury myself within the walls of the estate, seeing to the needs of it and my mother and brother and naught else." He shrugged. "I can be too focused on duty at times."

Bingley laughed. "Darcy can be the same."

"He speaks the truth," Darcy agreed. "Until recently I had only considered marriage in the light of duty just as I considered everything else."

Sir Matthew smiled knowingly. "You have found a lady who makes you question your view of duty, have you?"

"Indeed, I have," Darcy replied.

"I wish you joy," Sir Matthew said.

"I have not won her yet. In fact, I am not entirely certain I will win her."

"He will," said Bingley emphatically. "I know he will."

Sir Matthew's head cocked to the side, and curiosity suffused his expression. "I should enjoy hearing the tale, but I will not ask as it is not my place to be informed of your private matters," he said. "I will only wish you success."

"And I shall wish you the same," Darcy returned. "Do you have anyone in mind for the position of Lady Broadhurst?"

Sir Matthew shook his head. "I do not. It is perhaps unkind of me to say, but the few ladies I have met have been nothing more than a pretty face with feathers for brains." He shook his head. "Such giggling!"

"What do you wish for in a wife?" Darcy asked, casting a sidelong glance at Bingley.

Sir Matthew shrugged. "I likely know better what I do not want than what I want. I suppose I should like someone who would be a good hostess and manager."

"Does she have to be a gentleman's daughter?" Bingley asked pointedly. Caroline was proficient both at hosting soirees and managing everyone's affairs.

"You wish to be rid of a sister?" Sir Matthew asked with a laugh.

The man did not lack perception. That was a point in his favour according to Bingley. He would need to be a man who could see through Caroline's scheming and airs.

"I do."

Sir Matthew eyed Bingley cautiously. "What is wrong with her?" he asked.

Bingley chuckled. "I am not certain I should answer that, for we have had a falling out recently over her disapproval of my choice of bride, and even though she is my sister, I do not know that I would be the most charitable of persons to describe her."

"You are to be married?"

"Eventually," Bingley replied. "As soon as I can rid myself of a sister and help Darcy secure his heart's desire."

Poor Sir Matthew could not hide his confusion, though he did an admirable job in trying to disguise it.

"We are attending the Taylor's ball this evening," Bingley said. "Caroline will be there. You can meet her and judge for yourself if you might be persuaded to consider her."

"She is not hideous," Bingley added in response to Sir Matthew's continued look of skepticism.

"No," Darcy agreed. "She is quite handsome." He smirked. "She has the same colouring as her brother, but is much, much prettier."

Sir Matthew's features relaxed into a smile at the

comment. "Very well, if it is just a meeting," he agreed.

"It is just a meeting," Bingley assured him. "And if you are interested, then I will explain over a bottle of Darcy's finest port how both my happiness and that of Darcy hinges on my sister."

"My port?" Darcy said in surprise.

Bingley shrugged. "Very well, we will discuss it at my house over the best I have." He turned to Sir Matthew. "Do we have an agreement?" He held up his hand. "I neglected to mention she has twenty thousand pounds. She does not come empty-handed."

Sir Matthew drew his horse to a stop. "Yes," he said, nodding his head. "Yes, we have an agreement. I will meet your sister and then, if I find her to my liking, you may attempt to persuade me to aid your cause." He held out his hand, which Bingley gave a hearty shake, sealing the deal.

Chapter 10

Mr. Bennet popped his head out of his study door. "Hill."

"Yes, sir."

"Please inform Lizzy that I would like to see her." He held a very interesting missive in his hand and knew that his daughter had also received some correspondence from town. He was interested to know what Jane and Mrs. Gardiner had to say.

He closed the door and returned to his chair. He propped his feet on a footstool and peered through his glasses once again at Edward Gardiner's surprising letter, giving it a quick perusal and then putting it aside to open the next unexpected piece of mail. Colonel Fitzwilliam? The name did not sound familiar to him at all.

He smoothed the creases out of the letter and began reading.

Mr. Bennet,

Allow me to introduce myself to you. I am the Right Honorable Richard Fitzwilliam, colonel in his majesty's armed forces and second son of the Earl of Matlock. I am also the cousin of Fitzwilliam Darcy of Pemberley in Derbyshire, whose acquaintance you hold, and am the co-guardian of his sister.

What follows is information that is of a very sensitive nature, and I would request that as a gentleman you guard it with the utmost care.

Darcy has made me aware of the presence in your neighbourhood of a particular scoundrel with a well-practiced charm and ease of manner which will ingratiate him with nearly one and all. However, he is not to be trusted with credit, cards, or the hearts and virtue of young ladies.

Mr. Wickham is, as he will doubtless present himself, an acquaintance of the Darcy family and has been for many years. His father was my uncle's steward and a fine, upstanding man. His son has not been blessed with the same stalwart character.

While Mr. Wickham's father served the late Mr. Darcy well, treating him with the respect due to one of his station, Mr. Wickham has treated my cousins poorly and has tarnished the memories of both the late Mr. Darcy and his own father.

There is much history into which we could delve but suffice it to say that W. was a favourite of my uncle, and in homage to the service W's father had provided for Pemberley, my uncle bequeathed W a legacy of one thousand pounds and held for him the living that was in my uncle's power to bestow. The living was to be given upon there being a vacancy and W's taking orders. However, W did not wish to take orders but instead petitioned to be allowed to study the law. My cousin Darcy gave him three thousand pounds in lieu of the living. As it turns out, the law did not agree with W, and he spent his time and fortune in licentious living. When his funds had all been squandered, he returned to Darcy to request that he be allowed the living, which had just fallen open. Darcy refused based on the former arrangement of money in exchange for the living as well as the knowledge that W's lifestyle was not fitting for a man of the cloth. As you may well imagine, W was furious and abused my cousin severely.

Darcy thought that this would be his last interaction with the man, but alas, it was not. And this is the portion of the tale that I impart with trepidation. The sharing of the above is of little significance. However, what I share now is of a graveness that as a father I am certain you will appreciate.

It was just this past spring when W made his appearance and attempted to exact his revenge on Darcy. While Miss Darcy was in Ramsgate with her companion, a woman we later discovered was a friend of W's, Wickham played upon her tender heart and aroused her affection with the goal of persuading her to elope with him, thereby acquiring her thirty thousand and ensuring the misery of her brother. Thankfully, Darcy arrived before the scheme could be set into motion, and his sister confessed the whole of the matter to him. Once again, Wickham did not leave my cousin's presence on friendly terms as you can well imagine.

He is a profligate and a gambler who will likely

leave Hertfordshire with many unpaid debts and quite likely a few ruined maids.

I am given to understand, by my cousin's account and that of Mr. Bingley, that you have several pretty daughters. I know that they do not have a fortune equal to what Miss Darcy has, but one of them has something that money cannot buy and would make her of great interest to W. – my cousin's admiration. The possibility of separating Darcy from a lady he admires would please W immensely.

I have written a letter to Colonel Forster regarding W's propensity to dally with the ladies and be less than genuine with the merchants. I have done all this at my cousin's request as he does not wish to see the residents of Hertfordshire harmed by Wickham. He would have made his case known while in the area if it were not for fear of Miss Darcy's folly being exposed and his fear that he could not calmly and rationally relate his knowledge of the man since the wound caused to his sister is still not one which has healed.

Again, I would petition you, as both a gentleman and a father, to protect this information. Please *notify either myself or Darcy should any merchant find that he has fallen prey to Wickham's liberty in purchasing and lack of the same in paying his debts. Darcy has given his word that he will settle such accounts should the need arise.*

God Bless,

R.F.

Mr. Bennet sank back in his chair. First, he had received a missive from Gardiner mentioning both that there were wealthy and upstanding gentleman who admired and wished to court his eldest daughters and that there was a man in the militia of whom he should be cautious, and now this letter repeated much of what he had heard though it delved more deeply into the harm that Wickham had caused the Darcy family. He shook his head. He could not pass such damaging information off as being the dislike of one man to another, for what gentleman would place his sister's reputation in such a potentially damaging position without cause?

"Come," he called in response to the knock at his door.

"Hill said you wished to see me." Elizabeth entered and took a seat near her father.

He nodded and gave her a fleeting glance. His mind was still turning over the information he had just read. He placed the letter in his hand next to the one from Mr. Gardiner on the desk. "I understand you received a letter from Jane. How is she?"

Elizabeth drew a folded piece of paper from her pocket. "You may read it."

He shook his head. "I trust you to tell me all that I must know. Has Mr. Bingley called on her?"

"He has!"

Mr. Bennet loved the way Elizabeth's face would shine when she smiled as she was now. He watched as her brows furrowed, and the smile faded into puzzlement.

"It is the strangest thing," she said as she unfolded her letter.

"How so?" He was certain he knew what or, more precisely, who made Mr. Bingley's call strange.

"Mr. Darcy called with him."

Mr. Bennet feigned surprise. "He did? Is he interested in courting Jane?" He bit back a smile as his second eldest daughter shook her head and looked at him with more confused astonishment than he had ever seen on her face. Perhaps Mr. Darcy would be good for her if he could challenge her way of thinking as he seemed to be doing. Elizabeth needed a husband with a keen mind and a will that was not easily bent. From what he had gathered of the man while out hunting, Mr. Darcy seemed to possess both fortitude and intelligence.

"According to Aunt Gardiner, he hopes to court me."

"He is not Mr. Collins, and you must eventually marry." Mr. Bennet chuckled as Elizabeth's eyes grew wide. "He is a worthy gentleman, my dear."

Elizabeth shook her head. "You do not find him disagreeable?"

Her father shrugged. "He has a tendency to be dour, or so it seems. However, our acquaintance was of a short duration, and we do not know what he would be like at his own home." Her head cocked to the side, and he knew that he had likely gone too far in his acceptance of the man.

"What are you not telling me?"

He chuckled. She was perceptive even in her current befuddled state. "I have received two missives of my own with some startling information in them. However, before I share them with you, I must tell you that I am sending you to your aunt and uncle."

"Why?" Caution — or was it trepidation that coloured her tone? Whichever it was, it caused Mr. Bennet's lips to twitch in suppressed amusement. She was such a delight!

"Ten thousand a year is not a sum of money a lady refuses without due diligence in deciphering a gentleman's character."

Elizabeth's mouth snapped closed. "You would have me marry him?"

He shook his head. "No, I would have you make an informed choice." He passed her the two letters that lay on his desk. "One is from your uncle, and the other is from Colonel Fitzwilliam."

She blinked and looked at her father in confusion.

"He introduces himself far better than I ever could," he replied with a wink.

She began reading the colonel's letter just as he knew she would. If any of the information in any of the four letters they held between them were to sway her opinion of Mr. Darcy and provide the man with a second chance, it was the colonel's letter. "It seems our Mr. Darcy might have had just reason to be so unpleasant."

He settled back and watched her face as she read the letter twice before proceeding to read her uncle's letter.

"It seems Jane will be married soon," he said as she began reading the second letter. "And you could be as well."

Upon completion of her perusal of both letters, Elizabeth flopped back in her chair and expelled a whoosh of air.

"What say you?" her father asked.

Her head shook slowly from side to side. "I do not know what to say." She handed him the letters she had received from Jane and her aunt. "The Mr. Darcy described in these letters is not the Mr. Darcy I met." Her brows drew together. "Can Mr. Wickham be so bad?"

Her father shrugged. "It appears he can be."

Another whoosh of air escaped her.

"Your aunt and Jane have both included an apology from Mr. Darcy for his words at the assembly?"

Elizabeth nodded while one shoulder lifted and lowered in a small half shrug.

Mr. Bennet returned her letters to her and gathered his two from her. "You will not say anything about what you read in these." He knew she would not, but he felt he must say it.

"No, of course not." She folded her letters and put them back into her pocket. Then, she just sat there, her eyes fixed on the shelf of books behind her father.

Her head occasionally shook, and she grimaced, letting her father know that she was attempting to reason everything out while quite likely remonstrating herself for her lack of discernment about the character of not only Darcy but also Mr. Wickham. There was one thing in regard to that last gentleman that he needed to know. Elizabeth had spent a great deal of time in Wickham's company and seemed to enjoy it.

"I must ask," he began, "for I must know the full extent of things. Has Mr. Wickham touched your heart?"

Her eyes grew wide. "No, I counted him a friend but naught else." She shook her head once again. "However, it appears he might not have even been that."

"Sadly, yes." Mr. Bennet drew a deep breath and expelled it. "I found him very pleasant and had thought he might even make a good son." He shrugged. "But, I would not consign any of my daughters to a marriage with one who can squander money as readily as it seems he does."

Elizabeth nodded.

"You may go. I can see you need time to ponder."

Elizabeth rose slowly from her chair and moved toward the door, but she turned back instead of opening the door and exiting as her father expected. "Mr. Darcy admires me?"

There was so much disbelief in her tone that it caused his heart to pinch at the thought of not having her here to visit him in his study. However, Derbyshire was not so very far away. What was a couple days journey when it took you to where your child resided?

"It appears he does."

Her lips curled upwards, likely of their own accord since the expression in her eyes was still distant.

"I will take you to town myself," he said, causing her eyes to become focused and her lashes to flutter in surprise. "Tell your aunt that we will arrive in a se'nnight. And not a word to your mother about Mr. Bingley. I shall tell her that news when it is closer to our time to depart. Jane does not need her mother descending upon her or her Mr. Bingley before the papers are signed." He chuckled at the way Elizabeth rolled her eyes and shook her head. "Nor do we wish her to know that there is a gentleman with ten thousand a year who would like to persuade another one of her daughters into the matrimonial state."

"Papa!" Elizabeth chided.

"I am merely stating things as I see them. Now, off with you to consider what you have learned and to decide if your old papa is correct in his suppositions." He waved her away. "I look forward to hearing your conclusions," he called as she pulled the door shut behind her, and he was left to consider for himself the truth of two daughters married.

Chapter 11

While Elizabeth considered what to make of the letters that she had read, Darcy and Bingley were introducing Sir Matthew Broadhurst to Caroline. They did not do so directly, of course. Bingley was still not on speaking terms with his sister, and she was equally as put out with him.

"Hurst," Bingley greeted his brother-in-law as he sat down at the table which had just been vacated by the men who had been playing cards with Mr. Hurst.

Hurst grunted something of a greeting. "I cannot tolerate her." He waved his glass at a footman for a refill. "Louisa, I can abide on most days, but Caroline?" He shook his head. "And she does not have a pleasing effect on her sister. It is not right that I should be saddled with both of your sisters." He took a large gulp from his fresh glass of port.

"She is here?" Bingley asked calmly. He could understand the man's displeasure. Caroline was demanding and often in a foul mood if things were not done as she wished them done. He could only imagine just how cantankerous Caroline was at present with her spending curtailed, her residence moved, and her schemes to see him married to one of her friends at an end.

"She will be at any venue where there is a chance of foisting her off on some poor swain," he replied with no little amount of determination.

"Do you think you could pretend she is not the extreme burden she is for a few moments?" Hurst in his current state would be of no help in convincing Sir Matthew to meet Caroline.

Hurst lifted a skeptical brow. "Is there a good reason for such a performance?"

Bingley smiled and nodded as he settled back into his chair. "Indeed, there is. His name is Sir Matthew Broadhurst."

Hurst's head tipped to the side, and his glass returned to the table without a drop of its contents being consumed. "Continue."

"Sir Matthew is in need of wife before he can claim the entirety of his inheritance. We are in need of someone – anyone – to marry Caroline. He is willing to meet her, but I am sure you can see how my introducing him to her would not make his acceptance a possibility of even minuscule size."

Leaning back in his chair and wearing a half-pleased expression, Hurst cradled his port in his hand, taking a small sip before stating what both men knew to be true. "She'll not have him no matter who introduces him to her. He's not Darcy."

"She will never have Darcy."

"Aye, we both know that, but she's as daft as a duck trying to swim in a frozen pond."

Bingley chuckled. Caroline was not a fool about everything. However, when it came to her ambitions to gain Pemberley, she made the residents of Bedlam seem perfectly rational.

"Does he know she will not come willingly?" There was a calculating look in Hurst's eyes that Bingley had expected to see. Hurst was not without the ability and desire to scheme himself into better circumstances, and Bingley knew that being relieved of Caroline as a house guest was the best circumstance that could occur at the moment.

"He is only meeting her. He has not agreed to

take her off our hands just yet," Bingley cautioned. "Hence the need to tread carefully."

"Aye, let me meet the fellow. I shall not hide her flaws, but I will not parade them before the man either."

Bingley looked toward the door and nodded to Darcy. "The sooner we get on with this business the better, do you not think?" Bingley replied to Hurst's startled look as Darcy and Sir Matthew approached. "She is never returning to my house."

Hurst scowled and then smiled. "Tie 'er up and toss her in a carriage bound for Gretna Green on the hour."

"Perhaps we should not move quite so quickly as that," Bingley replied with a laugh.

"You only say that because she is not at your house," muttered Hurst.

"Sir Matthew, my brother, Mr. Reginald Hurst. Hurst, Sir Matthew Broadhurst of Stoningham in Surrey. I have explained to Hurst that you would like an introduction to Caroline, and he is willing to provide you the service."

"Anxious to be rid of her?" Sir Matthew asked pointedly.

"Like the pox," Hurst grumbled.

Bingley gave his brother's shin a solid kick.

"I prefer to have my wife to myself," Hurst added, moving his legs outside the range of Bingley's boot.

Sir Matthew's expression grew grave. "I am no fool. I know if both brothers and a good friend of the family wishes to be rid of a lady, there is a reason, and that reason must have to do with a deficiency of some sort."

Hurst sighed and lifted his glass to his lips, taking a swallow before continuing. "She is determined to have Darcy," he said. "And like a filly who wishes for the grass in the meadow rather than the feed in the stall, she is stubborn and kicking against the constraints of reality."

"That is no doubt part of what you wished to tell me if this meeting between myself and Miss Bingley is to my liking?" he asked Bingley.

Bingley nodded. "I did not wish to drag Darcy's situation out to just anyone, but yes."

"A harridan?"

Bingley's heart sank at the word. How would he ever persuade a chap to take on Caroline? She was every inch a harridan.

"She's not always been," said Hurst. "She just

has the notion in her head that she is going to marry Darcy and rise above her roots. She can be very agreeable about most other things. She does like to have her way and can cause a scene if she does not get it, but she is among the most accomplished ladies as you will find." He placed his glass on the table and, leaning forward, put up a finger to punctuate his point. "And you must remember that she has been training herself to be the mistress of Pemberley, which is no small estate. I do not know your estate, but I dare say she could have it ticking along like a newly wound clock."

"But a bit of a harridan?"

"Yes," said Darcy.

"Needs redirecting?"

Darcy nodded. "Please, I beg you."

Sir Matthew chuckled. "Dead set against her as a wife, are you?"

"Yes."

"He has his eye on a pretty little thing from Hertfordshire." Hurst took another drink of his port. "She is much better suited to Darcy than Caroline." He shrugged. "I am not always sleeping," he said with a wink. "Now, shall we play a game first or get straight to it?"

"I am not much of a card player," Sir Matthew admitted.

"Do you dance?" Hurst asked as he rose.

"I actually enjoy the activity. I have an affinity for music, you see."

Hurst's brows rose. "Caroline does like music." He gave the man next to him an appraising look. "You're handsome and you have a title, so those will stand you in good stead." He paused. "She is a schemer at times. How stalwart are you?"

"My mother has often said there are few less yielding than I, but I cannot see it." The corner of his lips tipped upward in amusement.

"Then, you will do fine," said Hurst, clapping Sir Matthew on the shoulder. "I should hate to present her with anyone weaker than immovable."

"Since you have not run away at such a comment, then I am to assume you are not easily frightened," said Bingley with a laugh.

"It is just a meeting," Sir Matthew reminded them.

"We are a hopeful lot," said Hurst.

"Or desperate," said Sir Matthew with a grin.

"Aye, there is that," Hurst agreed. "I wish my wife to run my house and not my sister, but that is neither here nor there at the moment. Come along, Sir Matthew. Let's see how you like her."

"No matter how this meeting goes, I will call on you gentlemen in three hours time. That should give me enough of an opportunity to have danced with her and watched her with others."

"We will await your arrival with eager anticipation," said Bingley. Then, he and Darcy slipped out of the Taylor's ball, for neither wished for their presence to place any hindrance on this meeting.

Bingley blew out a breath as his carriage pulled away from the curb. "Our happiness could be closer to our grasp in three hours."

"Or just as remote," Darcy added, causing Bingley to shake his head and chuckle.

~*~*~

Three hours later, just as promised, Sir Matthew arrived at Bingley's home and was shown to the study. Glasses of port were poured, and the four gentlemen settled in front of the hearth where a fire burned brightly, driving away shadows and filling the room with welcome warmth.

It was four gentlemen, not just three, for Richard had called at Bingley's and discovered that Sir Matthew was arriving later and could not be persuaded to leave under any circumstances, save for a man from his unit delivering orders that needed immediate attention. And since no such man appeared with said orders, he had waited with an open book on his knee and his head resting against the back of his chair while he dozed. Darcy, knowing how ill his cousin tended to sleep at night, kept his voice low while he and Bingley pondered the future and recalled the past.

"So?" Bingley's question cut through the air of anxious anticipation which hung in the air.

"I wish to know more about your situation and that of Darcy's before I come to a conclusion," said Sir Matthew. "She is pretty just as you said," he said to Darcy. "There is that in her favour."

"What do you wish to know about Darcy?" Richard asked with a grin.

"I can speak for myself," Darcy retorted.

"Both you and Darcy said that you have your eyes on possible wives, did you not?" Sir Matthew directed the question to Bingley.

"That is correct," said Bingley. "As you know, my wealth comes from trade and was left to me by my father with the hope that I would use it to secure an estate and elevate my family. To that purpose, I leased Netherfield, an estate in Hertford-shire, at Michaelmas. Darcy joined me there to help me evaluate its condition and teach me some of what I will need to know."

"And this is where you met your lady?" Sir Matthew stretched his feet toward the fire.

"Yes, Miss Jane Bennet. Her father owns the estate next to Netherfield."

"A gentleman's daughter," Sir Matthew nodded in approval. "It seems just the sort of young lady one who is aspiring to be a gentleman should marry as she will know what is expected of her role as his wife."

"That is not why I chose her," Bingley said. "It frankly mattered not to me what her origins were. Miss Bennet is one of the most beautiful and kind ladies I have ever met."

Richard chuckled. "And Bingley is well-versed in beautiful ladies. His charm has gained him access where his ties to trade would keep him out."

"If only we all could be so fortunate," Sir Matthew said with a laugh. "I confess I do not pos-sess a great deal of charm. Never have and, most likely, never will."

"But you have a title," said Richard. "One does

not need copious amounts of charm if one has either a title or a fortune the size of Darcy's." He chuckled. "If you have both, as my brother the viscount does, then you could be the ugliest, grumpiest curmudgeon in all of the empire and have women flocking to you." He shook his head.

"Your brother is neither ugly nor a curmudgeon," Darcy argued.

"Aye, but the ladies do gather."

"He should marry and be done with it," said Sir Matthew. "He is not married, is he?"

"No, but my mother insists it happens this season, so by summer he may be."

"And then she will begin harassing you twice as much as she does now," said Bingley.

"I am hoping my brother refuses to comply." Richard drained the last of his port and rose to refill his glass. "But, we are not here to discuss my marital state," he said as he removed the stopper from the bottle. "Bingley, continue to tell Sir Matthew why your sister is set against Miss Bennet."

"Right. Miss Bennet. She is the eldest of five daughters."

"Five?" Sir Matthew said in surprise.

"No brothers," Darcy added.

"Indeed?"

Bingley nodded. "Five pretty daughters." He grinned. "Miss Mary might make an excellent Colonel's wife," he teased.

Richard shook his head. "Not unless she has a fortune. Remember, I am the second son, not the heir." He settled back into his chair.

"We are not here to see Miss Bennet's sisters married," said Darcy.

"One we are," Richard said into his glass as he lifted it to take a drink.

"Miss Elizabeth Bennet is the second eldest daughter and the lady who has captured Darcy's heart," Bingley explained. "And that is one reason why my sister is opposed to my marrying Miss Bennet. For if I am married to Miss Bennet, then, Darcy will necessarily be thrown into the path of Miss Elizabeth, and Caroline suspects that Darcy is besotted."

"Which he is," Darcy added.

"I do like hearing you admit it," Richard muttered.

"As do I," Darcy replied. "Miss Elizabeth is not the only objection Bingley's sister has raised. Miss

Bennet's family is..." He paused. "Well, there is no particularly polite way to say it. There are those of her family who are both ridiculous and improper at times. They also have an uncle who is a country solicitor and another who is a tradesman here in town. However, I do think these objections would be overlooked if I were to offer for Caroline. Then, she would willingly allow her brother to marry as he chooses." He sighed.

"She is so set, is she?" Sir Matthew asked.

Darcy nodded. "She has never attracted my attention in such a fashion. She is not what I wish for in a wife. We are not companionable."

"And companionship is important to you?" asked Sir Matthew.

"It is."

"I see." The port in Sir Matthew's glass swirled up and around and down, up and around and down, as he thought. "If you were to marry – both of you – and Miss Bingley remained single, why would that be an issue?"

"I would not wish to subject Miss Bennet to having to host her. I could see Caroline causing problems for my wife, resulting in misery for her. Miss Bennet has a sweet, tender constitution. She has already felt the sting of my sister's maneuverings. You see, when Caroline left Hertfordshire, she left a letter for Miss Bennet hinting at my marrying Darcy's sister. Not a word of it was true, of course. Then, when Miss Bennet came to town to visit her aunt and uncle in Gracechurch Street, she paid a call on my sisters. They did not deign to accept her into the house, and I am certain they have no intention of returning her call. A call, I might add, that she concealed from me. I only learned of it through Darcy."

Sir Matthew's head bobbed up and down slowly. "I see," he said once again before slipping back into thought as he watched his port chase itself along the sides of his glass. Then, the glass stilled. He drained its contents and placed it on the table. "Your sister has twenty thousand?"

"More if it is needed," said Bingley.

Sir Matthew smiled. "I am not agreeing to this for your money, but I do wish to have something to settle on children and such, you understand."

"You will take her?" Bingley asked hopefully.

Sir Matthew nodded. "I must marry to take possession of my full inheritance. The lady I met tonight was all that was proper, if a bit cool, in her reception. She mingled with ease amongst the other people in attendance. She did not want for dance partners. Her taste in fashion," he shook his head, "it is good but expensive. That could be an issue. I do not like to be separated from my money, for as you know, it is not my money to dispose of as I wish without thought. There is a duty to those who follow me. To my son who will take up the title. I know that such thinking is perhaps not popular, but it is how I believe."

He rose and picked up his glass. "May I?" he asked.

"Certainly," Bingley said.

"I like you," Sir Matthew said as he crossed to where the decanter of port rested on a cabinet. "You and Hurst have been very open with me about the trial your sister has presented to you, and you have not tried to dupe me into thinking I am tying myself to an angel when she is not." He turned and leaned against the cabinet. "I actually think we could do well together. I could be wrong, of course, and that does concern me for I have always longed for felicity in marriage." He shrugged. "I will call on her at Hurst's tomorrow and invite her to go for a drive. Her acceptance or reluctance of those items will tell us how we should proceed."

Bingley raised a brow.

"I am not opposed to a compromise," Sir Matthew said with a grin. "I see no point in delaying. I need a wife, and you gentlemen need to be free to claim yours without fear of reprisal."

"You will truly take her?"

Sir Matthew nodded. "I will not marry quickly. I will fall into a betrothal with haste, but I do wish for a bit of time to court her after she has been forced to accept such a courtship before we wed."

"Are you hoping that once she can no longer consider Darcy as an option due to whatever compromise we arrange, she will find her more rational self?" Richard asked.

"Indeed, I am," Sir Matthew said. "I would also rather not take an angry hornet home with me. Time should help me with that as well."

"You are a sly one." There was no mistaking the admiration in Richard's voice.

"So I have been told a time or two." Sir Matthew lifted his glass to his lips and hid a smile behind it. "If you are a quiet, focused sort of person, slyness is rarely suspected."

Richard guffawed. "Do you play cards?" he asked.

"Not often."

"But when you do, I suspect you win," Richard said.

"Indeed," Sir Matthew agreed. "Nearly always." He returned to his seat. "Do you wish to speak of marriage settlements now or after our betrothal becomes necessary."

Bingley shook his head and chuckled. "I am certain I am going to enjoy being your brother." He rose and went in search of paper and pen. "I see no reason to delay."

Chapter 12

"My home has never been so full of handsome eligible gentlemen." Mrs. Gardiner smiled broadly as she settled back into the chair from which she had been presiding over the discussion in her sitting room. "Sir Matthew, it is, of course, a delight to meet you."

Sir Matthew inclined his head in acceptance of her words. "I thank you for accepting me into your home with no prior introduction."

Mrs. Gardiner waved his words away. "Any friend of Mr. Bingley or Mr. Darcy is always welcome in my home."

Darcy thoroughly enjoyed how her eyes danced with pleasure as it once again reminded him of Elizabeth.

"I understand you are from Surrey?" Mrs. Gardiner continued.

"Yes, ma'am, I am."

Mrs. Gardiner did not reply but merely looked at him expectantly.

Sir Matthew straightened a sleeve. "My estate, or what will be my estate, is Stoningham. It was left to me by my uncle, along with the title. He was my father's older brother, but he never married. Therefore, the inheritance has fallen to me." He went on, at her prompting, to tell her about his mother, his sisters, and his brother. She even managed to wrangle out of him details about his sisters' families and situations.

"And you wish to share all this with Miss Bingley?" Mrs. Gardiner had risen to pour the tea which had just arrived.

"I need a wife," Sir Matthew replied.

Mrs. Gardiner replaced the teapot on its tray but did not lift the filled cup to pass to Jane, who stood ready to distribute the tea things. "You have met Miss Bingley?"

"I have."

"And you are satisfied?"

He nodded.

"And your family? Will they also be satisfied?"

He shrugged. "I believe my mother will be happy to have me married."

Mrs. Gardiner lifted the teacup and handed it to Jane. "I will be happy to have you married," she said with a laugh, "for I wish for nothing more than to see my nieces well-settled with these two fine gentlemen." She began filling another cup. "However, I would not be able to rest easy knowing that such a thing came about at the expense of your happiness." Her eyes met Jane's. "And I know Jane would also feel such a calamity most grievously, for her heart is amongst the tenderest in the land."

Jane smiled and blushed as she returned from giving Sir Matthew his tea to get another cup.

"You may rest assured, ladies, that I have considered my own happiness very carefully in all of this. I believe, in time, Miss Bingley and I will get on quite well." He hid a smile behind the rim of his cup. "After her sharp edges are smoothed a bit, that is."

"You do not go into this blindly, then?" Mrs. Gardiner asked.

"No, my eyes are fully open. I know there is a risk in what I am doing. A great risk. However, I am not the sort to gamble without thought."

"Very well," Mrs. Gardiner said as she handed Jane a cup of tea and then poured one for herself. "We will proceed with clear consciences."

"As you should," Sir Matthew agreed.

"You called on my sister today, did you not?" Bingley asked.

It was the topic Darcy had hoped to broach as soon as the man entered the room, but as it was not his home nor was it his sister's future being arranged, he had refrained, and instead, he had thoroughly enjoyed watching Mrs. Gardiner interrogate Sir Matthew while feeling quite glad that this time he was not the person of interest to Mrs. Gardiner.

"Mmm hmm." Sir Matthew nodded as he swallowed his tea. "She was agreeable. Very cordial. We had a good discussion, and I did ask her to go for a drive tomorrow." He paused, and his brows furrowed. "She has agreed but not with alacrity. I think she would have refused if Hurst had not entered the room just prior and made a point of gaining her attention with a cough when she did not immediately reply." He took another sip of his tea. "Drawing her along will take far too long. I think it best if we move toward limiting her choices to all but me. She can be convinced of my worth after she has accepted my offer."

There was a constant calmness about this man that Darcy was beginning to admire. There was a matter-of-factness to everything. Possible outcomes were presented – both good and bad – discussed and then put away like papers in folders, each with its own place. Even when Mrs. Gardiner had questioned him, he had replied with ease and directness. This unflappable, intelligent, calculating gentleman might actually be the making of Caroline Bingley. The thought brought a smile to his lips. Who would have ever thought there was such a gentleman? Darcy certainly had not until this moment.

"Then we need a plan," Bingley declared.

"I do not want to be implicated as the source of the compromise," Sir Matthew placed his empty cup on its saucer and set it aside on a table near him. "I do not wish to go into this marriage with any more difficulty laid at my door than necessary."

Darcy watched Mrs. Gardiner hide a smile. "That seems wise," he said.

Mrs. Gardiner nodded her head in ready agreement.

The room fell into silence for a moment, each occupied with his or her own thoughts.

"I should not mind being the source," said Jane.

All eyes turned toward her.

Though she bit her lip and her hands were clasped tightly, there was a sparkle in her eyes that Darcy found surprising, but then, the Jane he had met here in town had surprised him several times already.

"Are you certain?" Mrs. Gardiner asked.

Jane drew in a deliberate breath and pulled herself the tiniest degree more upright. "This whole thing was my idea. Any blame and displeasure which arise should be mine to bear." Her lips curled up slightly. "Besides, though I know it is not proper to seek a reprisal, I do find I would not mind causing Miss Bingley some discomfort, for she has caused plenty for me." Her smile grew. "And I would have her know that though I smile often and am obliging, I am not without resolve."

"That should stand you in good stead for after you are married," Sir Matthew said.

"Aye," said Bingley. "I am not opposed to sharing in Caroline's displeasure."

"Oh, no!" Mrs. Gardiner cried, clapping her

hands. "She might suspect you, and a scheme is much more effective if it is accomplished with an element or two of surprise. Jane's being involved will be surprising to Miss Bingley, no doubt, but not nearly so much so if the accident, whatever it may be, is affected with her brother's assistance, since that brother is currently put out with her." Her eyes shifted from Bingley to Darcy. "However..." Her voice trailed off and her eye brows raised. "That is," she added, "if assistance is needed?"

Darcy pointed at himself. "Me?"

Mrs. Gardiner nodded.

Darcy's brows furrowed as he pondered the thought for only a moment. "I am at your service, Miss Bennet. Do you have a plan?"

The sparkle in her eyes grew brighter as she nodded in reply.

"Then, tell me what to do."

Jane looked around the room at each person, then, leaning forward, said in a soft but conspiratorial voice. "First, I will need an invitation to a ball."

~*~*~

Less than a week later, Darcy stood before the Johnsons' grand townhouse, dressed in his finest.

It had not been so very difficult to secure the invitations needed to the Johnsons' ball. Mr. Johnson had been eager to assist Darcy with his plan. There was nothing the man seemed to like more than a cunning stratagem. And, Mrs. Johnson had been easily persuaded to part with a few invitations when her husband had suggested that Mr. Darcy's being in attendance would without a doubt guarantee that Colonel Fitzwilliam would attend as well as Mr. Bingley. However, he did not share with his wife the plan that was being laid to make her ball the most talked about ball of the season.

Richard huffed as he climbed out of Darcy's carriage. "You do realize that you are indebted to me for this, do you not?" He skewered both Darcy and Bingley, whose carriage stood behind Darcy's, with a displeased look.

Both men nodded.

"She better be worth it," he muttered.

"She is," Darcy said. "I just hope I can persuade her that I am worthy of her regard." He knew that his cousin was not entirely put out with having to dance two sets with Miss Johnson, for Richard had smirked and teased all week about Darcy finally causing a stir in the family by following his heart and not his sense of duty. "I think you will agree with me about her worth once you meet her. That is actually why you are here, is it not?"

Richard straightened his sleeves and did not look at Darcy. "I am not sure I understand your meaning."

Darcy chuckled. "Come, shall we get on with the introductions, so that your curiosity might be satisfied? You could have travelled here on your own and arrived fashionably late. There was no other need for you to arrive early with us, other than to meet Miss Elizabeth."

His cousin shrugged. It was as close to an admission as Darcy was likely to get. Richard was a curious sort and had, ever since meeting Miss Bennet, been keenly interested in meeting Miss Elizabeth.

"I am here to watch the theatrics," he replied as they approached the door to the townhouse.

"You do not wish to meet the future Mrs. Darcy?"

Bingley's question was met by a small growling noise.

"Admit it. You are curious," Bingley said with a laugh. "She has three other sisters," he whispered.

"Very well. I will admit to curiosity if you refrain

from attempting to marry me off to one and all. It is bad enough that I must dance twice with the same lady." He gave Darcy a pointed look. "There will be talk, and it will reach my mother."

"Your sacrifice is duly noted."

"Good. Now, lead me to the rare creature who has enchanted the dour and disapproving Fitzwilliam Darcy. I wish to know that my sacrifice is not in vain."

"Darcy, Bingley, Fitzwilliam." Mr. Johnson looked as eager as a schoolboy on Christmas day waiting for his Christmas pudding.

"Mr. Bennet and his daughters are in the library." His eyes twinkled. "My wife was called away to attend to something just as they arrived." His brows flicked upward. He nodded his head toward the interior of the house and began walking in the direction of the library. "Quickly, while she attends to another emergency."

Reaching their destination, Mr. Johnson opened the door. "Mr. Bennet, Miss Bennet, Miss Elizabeth, your gentlemen have arrived." Turning to the gentlemen behind him, he added, "I can see why you are so determined to be rid of your sister, Mr. Bingley. Miss Bennet is quite the beauty and her sister?" His eyebrows flicked up as he looked at Darcy. "Well worth a bit of scheming. She's delightful." Then, before allowing them entrance to the room, he said, "My Marietta is still unattached, Colonel."

Richard shook his head. "I will dance my two, but I am attached to my commission at present."

"Ah, well," the man said as he stepped aside, "you cannot fault a father for trying."

"No," Richard agreed. "I would fault him if he did not."

Darcy and Bingley were both inside the library before Richard had finished his exchange with Mr. Johnson.

"Colonel, it is good to see you," Jane greeted as he entered the room. "Thank you for helping us with this plan."

"It is my pleasure to be of service."

Jane lifted a brow, and her lips curled upwards in amusement.

"A small prevarication," he whispered, causing her to laugh.

"Colonel, I would like you to meet my father, Mr. Thomas Bennet. Father, this is the Right Honourable Colonel Richard Fitzwilliam."

"Ah, so I do get to meet the writer of the letter. I thank you, sir, for alerting me to the true nature of Mr. Wickham."

"I cannot say it was my pleasure that it was necessary to impart such information, but I am glad it has been welcomed."

Mr. Bennet nodded. "It is never easy to relate unpleasant news, which makes it all the more appreciated. I have shared it only with my Lizzy." He drew the pretty lady next to him forward. "Colonel Fitzwilliam, this is my second daughter, Elizabeth."

Richard bowed. "I am delighted to finally meet you." He glanced at his cousin. "I have heard much about you."

"Aside from what I could glean from your letter, I know very little about you," Elizabeth replied with a smile.

"There is very little to know," he assured her. "I am but a poor soldier."

Elizabeth laughed. "Yes, a Right Honourable poor soldier."

Richard shrugged. "Far poorer than I wish to be."

"We could all say that," said Mr. Bennet with a chuckle.

"I should very much like to sit for a while," Jane interrupted before Richard could reply. She took her father's arm and gave it a soft tug while she caught Darcy's eye and tipped her head toward her sister.

Darcy nodded. "Would you care to take a turn around the room?" he asked Elizabeth. "I am no Miss Bingley, but I do think I can circle a library just as well."

Elizabeth smiled, though her brow furrowed. Jane had claimed that the Mr. Darcy she had met in town was different from the one she had met in Hertfordshire, and it appeared she was right. This Mr. Darcy seemed nearly at ease. "I should like that, Mr. Darcy."

"Allow me to begin our conversation with a long overdue apology," he said as she placed her hand on the arm he offered her. "I behaved abominably while at Netherfield. I had my reasons and considered myself justified. However, there is no justification for such poor behaviour." He drew a breath. "I slighted you, looked down on the neighbourhood, and connived to separate myself and Bingley from the area."

She was watching the floor before them.

"I should like to make reparations for my words and actions if you will allow it." He covered her hand with his, drawing her attention up from the red and orange of the carpet. "Can you forgive me?"

Elizabeth lifted her eyes from his hand to his face. "I can. Can you forgive me for listening to Mr. Wickham and speaking poorly of you?"

His smile as he nodded caused Elizabeth's breath to catch and her heart to flutter.

"Yes, yes, I can, and I am certain I deserved most of what you said about me."

"That does not make it right," she protested.

"I will allow that," he replied, "but it does make it understandable. My behavior is harder to comprehend."

They had made a full circuit of the room. Music was filtering in through the door, and they could hear people walking in the corridor.

"If we are to begin again," Darcy said softly, "then, allow me to ask you for a dance as I should have at our first meeting, for I cannot resist the temptation of your loveliness."

Chapter 13

"Have you concluded your thinking about Mr. Darcy yet?" Mr. Bennet asked as Elizabeth took a seat next to him in the library. She and he would make their appearance after the first set, so there was ample time for them to continue the discussion Mr. Bennet had begun when they had entered the carriage. There, he had questioned his daughter regarding her interactions with Mr. Darcy while he was in Hertfordshire, as well as how she might now consider the gentleman's behaviour in light of the secrets contained in Colonel Fitzwilliam's letter.

"He is so different."

"As Jane said."

Elizabeth nodded, perplexity was written across her face in the way her brows furrowed and how she pulled the right corner of her bottom lip between her teeth, and it was echoed in the way her shoulders rose and then drooped as she sighed.

Mr. Bennet knew that look and sigh well. His daughter was not good at admitting small faults. She had a propensity to strive to be absolutely correct at every turn, and it frustrated and angered her when she was not. He suspected that at present, his Lizzy was more than a trifle upset with herself and did not wish to admit it. It had been a trial to persuade her to admit that she had misjudged Mr. Darcy as they had travelled – not because Elizabeth had not realized that fact as soon as she had read the colonel's letter. No, she knew her error, she just did not wish to face the shame that came with the admission. Pride was never a pleasant partner. Eventually, it would demand its dues, and payment usually was extracted in the form of mortification.

"You like him," he offered to her the words he suspected she wished to say.

Her head bobbed up and down slowly. "I do, or I think I might."

Mr. Bennet sat quietly as his daughter pondered that thought for a moment.

"He was not at all proud just now." She stared

across the room toward the door. "He apologized." She turned her eyes to her father.

"For what?"

"For his comment at the assembly, how he behaved while in Hertfordshire, and for attempting to separate himself and Bingley from the area." Her head tipped to the side, and her eyebrows drew together.

Mr. Bennet chuckled. "Indeed, why would he attempt to separate himself from the area?"

Elizabeth blinked.

"Ah, my Lizzy, your eyes have always spoken to me. There was a flicker in them just now as you spoke of his leaving Hertfordshire." He patted her hand. "When your head tips after such a flicker, I know you are questioning something about whatever it was you were saying. I am not so unobservant as I appear." He sighed. "I should appear observant more often. For that, I must apologize. I have not done my duty as a husband and father." He straightened his waistcoat. "It is something I intend to correct, though I do fear I will not be successful. I am too given to taking my ease."

"Oh, Papa!"

"No, it is true. I do enjoy peace and solitude, and

though I love your mother and your sisters, they try my patience greatly." He shook his head. "What gentleman who is as fastidious as Mr. Darcy would wish to be tied to such a brood as mine?"

Elizabeth gasped.

"No, not you, my dear, nor Jane. I speak of your mother and younger sisters. They are precisely the opposite of Mr. Darcy, and I would venture to say he finds them as trying as I do. However, he lacks the love I have for them, for they are not his kin." His lips turned up in a small smile. "Yet."

He chuckled at her gasp. "I did tell you to consider it. I will not force you to marry against your wishes, but he is a sensible fellow, and he is not poor."

"Papa!"

"Be reasonable, my dear. You do not wish to be married to someone who will leave you in the hedgerows upon his demise. Such a worry can addle the mind."

"Oh, Papa." Elizabeth grasped his hand. "You will not leave us in the hedgerows. Mama exaggerates, does she not?"

His head bobbed up and down slowly as he gave her hand a reassuring squeeze. "She does, but knowing I cannot provide for her as I wish has been a heavy weight to bear. I tell you this because I would have you consider your future with your head as well as your heart." He squeezed her hand once again. "The man loves you. It is plain to see. And you are not indifferent to him. See how your cheeks grow rosy at the mere mention?" He chuckled. "Allow him to court you, Elizabeth. Study his character. Grow to like him more. I think you will be happy, but if I am wrong, do not accept his offer. However, I cannot allow you to shy away from this for fear of bearing reproof for not having judged fairly or some other foolish and proud reason without doing my best to persuade you to give Mr. Darcy a second chance. I love you far too much to do that, even if it means eventually having to give you away. Promise me you will consider what I have said."

Elizabeth's lips quivered, and her eyes filled with tears. "I will," she promised him.

He squeezed her hand once more. "Good, now before we become even more missish and you become a watering pot, we should take our places to observe the proceeding. Hopefully, there will be a few gentlemen left to partner you for dances.

Your mother would be rightfully put out with me for not having you dance every set with someone. To think you are here in town with so many wealthy young men and instead of dancing, your father has you sitting in a library."

Elizabeth laughed. "It is not you who has us sitting here; it is Jane."

"Of all my daughters, I never thought it would be my Jane scheming her way into a betrothal," he said with a laugh as he stood. "But then, it seems many people are not the same in town as they are in Hertfordshire."

"Except Miss Bingley," Elizabeth added with a smirk, causing her father to laugh again as she took his arm. "I am curious to meet this Sir Matthew," she whispered as they crossed the room. "Who would willingly wish to marry her?"

Her father winked. "We shall soon see, shall we not?"

"Indeed, we shall."

~*~*~

Jane took her place at Mr. Darcy's side, her hand on his arm, while Mr. Bingley followed Mr. Johnson down the corridor and into the ballroom from a door that would not draw notice. It was the same door through which her father would later enter with Elizabeth. Later – after Caroline's fate had been sealed.

Jane blew out a breath. Her heart was racing. She had never caused even a small stir at a ball before this, but she knew that entering the ballroom with Mr. Darcy was just the beginning of the attention she would draw this evening. She scanned the room as she entered. The light from numerous candles sparkled from the chandeliers and danced from mirror to mirror. Everything from the arrangement of the plants and chairs to the size of the floor and the number of musicians in the alcove was breathtaking. Everything was so much finer than anything she had experienced in Hertfordshire. The opulence and number of people in attendance at this ball even outshone Netherfield.

"Are you ready?" Darcy whispered.

She gave a small nod of her head and allowed him to lead her into the room. They circled to the left, passing a window with a set of chairs tucked into its alcove.

"She is just ahead of us," Darcy whispered.

"And Sir Matthew?" Jane attempted to peer through the crowd to where Mr. Darcy was looking, but he, having the greater height, had the advantage, and she would have to rely on his information for the time being.

"He appears to be just approaching to collect her for a dance."

"Precisely on schedule," Jane muttered.

"I do admire that about the man," Darcy replied.

Jane smiled and turned impertinent eyes up toward him. "As do I. Although I find his most endearing quality is his willingness to marry Miss Bingley."

"Indeed," Darcy agreed with a chuckle. "Here we go. Three steps and she will see us."

There was a hint of glee in Mr. Darcy's voice that surprised Jane, though only slightly. She had come to know the gentleman better since her arrival in town. He was not so dour as he had at first appeared. He was proper and given to meticulousness, but he was not without a playful bent. It might not be displayed so often as some such as Mr. Bingley might display such an inclination, but it was there, and it was delightfully surprising every time he displayed it. Elizabeth would be glad for it, and Jane suspected, her sister would likely draw that part of Mr. Darcy's character out. They would do well together, and from the way Elizabeth had fidgeted while waiting in the library and from how she welcomed Mr. Darcy tonight, Jane was certain that her sister was not unaffected by the gentleman – despite her pleas as they had talked last night that she was uncertain how she thought or felt about Mr. Darcy.

Jane heard her quarry before she saw her. The gasp Miss Bingley uttered was exceptionally pleasing.

"Miss Bingley, Mrs. Hurst," Darcy said in greeting. He looked blankly at Sir Matthew. "Have we met?"

For a man who despised all forms of disguise, Mr. Darcy seemed rather adept at prevarication.

"Sir Matthew Broadhurst of Stoningham in Surrey," Sir Matthew replied with a bow after which Darcy introduced himself and then Jane.

"A delight to meet you both."

Sir Matthew's expression was pleasant, and, if Jane were not mistaken, there was a glint of amusement in his eyes. He seemed to be enjoying himself, which was good since Jane still worried that she was asking him to take on a life of misery by marrying Caroline Bingley. Oh, she knew what he had said about knowing what he was taking on, but still, her heart was not wholly at ease.

"You did not tell me you had such a lovely friend," he said to Caroline. "Miss Bennet, I am promised to Miss Bingley for this set, but I would be honoured if you would allow me to claim the next dance. Unless, of course, it is already spoken for?"

"I am afraid the next set has been claimed, but perhaps the one after that?" Jane replied.

Sir Matthew knew right well that Mr. Bingley had claimed the set after the one with Mr. Darcy. These gentlemen, who seemed so honourable, were surprisingly good actors, and for that, Jane was exceedingly glad.

Caroline narrowed her eyes at Jane and stepped closer to Sir Matthew while casting an expectant glance at Darcy.

"I see someone to whom I wish to introduce you, and then we must find your father so that he does not think I have absconded with you," Darcy said to Jane. "I hope you ladies have a pleasant evening." He gave a small bow and led Jane away toward where Mr. Johnson was standing with Richard and a pretty young lady, whom, Jane guessed, was Miss Johnson. The colonel and Miss Johnson did seem to look well together.

"Miss Bingley did not look pleased when I did not request a dance, did she?" Darcy asked.

Again, there was that note of glee in his voice. "No, she did not, and did you notice how she attempted to lay claim to Sir Matthew when he requested a dance from me?"

Darcy chuckled. "Just as you said she would. You are very clever, Miss Bennet."

'Thank you," Jane replied with a smile. She was often complimented for her beauty but rarely for her wit. Cleverness was Lizzy's forte, so it was gratifying, for once, to be commended for intelligence and not beauty. "You played your part admirably."

Darcy inclined his head in acceptance of her praise.

They had reached Mr. Johnson and, therefore, their discussion ended. Jane was introduced to Miss Johnson and, for effect, the colonel. Then, as the musicians began to play, she, Darcy, Miss Johnson, and Richard took their places in the group of dancers with Caroline and Sir Matthew.

"Are you well?" Darcy asked as he took his place next to her.

Jane smiled. "I am. Are you?"

He gave a sharp nod of his head.

Jane looked across the circle to where Sir Matthew stood. She smiled but allowed her eyes to carry her question. He returned her smile as he gave her a slight nod. Gathering her fortitude as the first notes of the song began, she turned and curtseyed to the gentleman on her right before turning to Darcy on her left. Then she skipped and hopped her way through the steps, pausing to watch as others took their turns.

Finally, the ladies joined hands and went around in a circle in one direction and then the other. Jane's heart was beating far faster than the dance steps dictated as Darcy took the hand which was not holding Caroline's.

As she skipped towards him the second time, he gave her a tug causing her hand to slip from Caroline's. She stumbled slightly but being prepared for it, she did not fall. Caroline, however, was not so fortunate and found herself clasped tightly to Sir Matthew's chest as they tumbled to the floor.

"Are you injured?" Sir Matthew asked.

"Let me up," Caroline demanded, wiggling to break free of his hold.

"Not until I know you are uninjured," Sir Matthew said.

"I am well," Caroline sputtered.

"Are you certain?" Sir Matthew smoothed an imaginary hair from Caroline's cheek as his other arm clasped her firmly in place on top of him. "You look flushed."

"Let me up," Caroline insisted once more.

"You are very light," Sir Matthew said.

Caroline's eyes grew wide.

"Allow me to help you." Jane extended a hand to Caroline. "I feel just dreadful that I lost my grip."

"Do not touch me," Caroline hissed.

Jane drew her hand back. "Very well. I do apologize, Sir Matthew."

Sir Matthew smiled up at her. "No harm done."

"No harm done?" Caroline sputtered as he finally released her and allowed her to scramble off of him.

"That is what I said." Sir Matthew rose from the floor and brushed his breeches and then his sleeves before tugging on his waistcoat. "I am in need of a wife, and you will do nicely."

"A wife?" Caroline squeaked.

"Yes, as well as a mistress for my estate – it is

quite large — and mother for my children – we will need to have at least two. Boys preferably."

"I see no reason to not let you have her."

Caroline spun around. "Charles, be reasonable. It was a stumble, a misstep."

Bingley nodded. "Indeed, it was. A very fortuitous one." He took Jane's hand and pulled her to his side. "I'll expect you in my study tomorrow," he said to Sir Matthew. "Hurst," he said to his brother-in-law, who had just ambled up with Louisa, "Caroline is getting married."

"I am not." Caroline crossed her arms and glared at him.

"You do not wish for a large estate and fortune?" Hurst asked in surprise. "I had thought that was precisely what you were looking for. I am certain I have heard you declare such to your sister on many occasions. True, it is not Pemberley, but I hear Stoningham is impressive."

"Reginald," Louisa whispered loudly. "She is not a fortune hunter."

Hurst harrumphed. "Is she not?"

"Stop speaking. I shall be ruined," Caroline whispered.

"No," said Bingley, "you shall be married." He

nodded toward the door. "Shall we continue this discussion in the library?"

"Certainly," Sir Matthew agreed, taking Caroline's elbow and gripping it firmly as she attempted to pull it away from him. "Smile and look as if you are pleased," he whispered, "that is what you want them to comment on when you are gone rather than calling you all manner of unpleasant things."

Caroline stared at him for a moment, then, smiled. "Of course, my dear, you are correct. I was merely rattled by the fall." She lifted her right foot. "In fact, I believe, I have injured myself after all. If you would be so good as to allow me to lean on you until I can find a place to rest."

"Ah, see. That was not so difficult, was it?" he replied as she wrapped her arm around his.

Jane gave Bingley's hand a final squeeze and then released it.

Bingley shook his head and extended his hand to her again. "Come with me."

Jane looked at Mr. Darcy. "Do you mind?"

Darcy shook his head as a grin split his face. "I have never much cared for dancing, and besides, there is someone standing by that door over there whom, if I am to dance, I would dearly like to have as my partner."

Jane followed Darcy's gaze to where Elizabeth stood with her father. "I wish you well," she said as she took Bingley's arm. "Remember to tell her – "

"I know," Darcy interrupted. "I shall do my best not to blunder."

Chapter 14

"Miss Elizabeth, I believe the next set is ours," Darcy said as he came to stand with her and her father. "However, we must wait for this set to conclude." It was perhaps the first time he had ever wished for a dance to begin quickly rather than dreading the moment when he would have to place himself across from a lady and present himself as charmingly as he was able, which, in all honestly, was a meager offering on most occasions.

"That was as fine a performance as any I have seen," said Mr. Bennet. "I had not thought you the actor sort, but it appears I am wrong." Amusement danced in the gentleman's eyes.

"I cannot say that I have ever aspired to the role of actor," Darcy admitted, although, it had not been deplorable to take part in the charade which had just transpired. That was rather surprising.

"We are all actors at times, are we not?" Elizabeth interjected.

Her eyes were sparkling in that transfixing way they always did when she began a debate. Darcy waited with eager anticipation for her to present her argument.

"I, for instance," she continued, "must perform my roles as daughter and sister as well as niece, cousin, and friend."

"But there is a truth to such roles," Darcy retorted, his lips twitching with the pleasure that accompanied refuting her claim with one of his own. "The actor who dons a smock and frolics about the stage becomes what he is not while you are you no matter if you are with friends or family. There is an element in each role you portray that is real. Your lines are not scripted nor are your emotions contrived."

"Well said," Mr. Bennet agreed.

"Perhaps." Elizabeth motioned to the dancers. The sparkling in her eyes had ignited into a spark, steady and sure. "Do you suppose that all of the ladies and gentlemen in attendance are presenting themselves as they truly are? How much of the genuine person is on display, and how much is hidden?

Will the lady who fears to have it known that she enjoys studying the stars rather than Mr. Ackermann's drawings reveal herself as she is or as she is expected to be? Will she enter into a conversation with quickness or will she defer? Will she appear to be happily amused by a gentleman's conversation about trivial matters or will she interject a subject of substance?"

She shifted a step away from her father and closer to him as she immersed herself completely in her thoughts.

"And what of the gentleman with an estate that is ailing and in need of propping up? Will he not hide the true state of his affairs? Will he pursue where his bank accounts lead, or will he chase after his heart?" She shook her head. "It is as the bard said. We are all players on this great stage of life."

"That is also well stated," Mr. Bennet agreed. "And I would add one additional thought. Is it not possible that the fellow who prances about a stage in tunic and tights finds a bit of himself in the role he portrays? Might he not find himself comparing his own character to the part he plays?"

Darcy looked from daughter to father and back. Their brows were furrowed in thought in an almost identical fashion while their eyes held no censure but only genuine curiosity – the sign of a quick and hungry mind.

"I will grant you may both be correct," he said. "There are, no doubt, many in attendance who are very unlike who they truly are. Some will have noble reasons for their performance while others seek nothing more than amusement and sport." He paused. "I must admit that I am not at ease enough in a crowd such as this to always act as I am. As much as I say I despise disguise, I find I am often hiding myself behind an austere mien."

"I had not meant to rebuke," Elizabeth said quickly.

"No, I do not believe you were," he assured her. "I am merely extending your suppositions and examining them closely, and as I do so, I find I must consider myself just as you considered your roles as sister, daughter, cousin, niece, and friend. However, in doing so, I find that my original rebuttal remains true. I am not given to frivolity. I tend to be more serious in nature. These things become part of the disguise but remain true to who I am. For another who gads about glibly, one might find that such a one is naturally more free-spirited, and therefore, when he presents himself, his exuberance is merely an extension of his true identity." He shrugged. "The same can be said for character flaws, I suppose. A person given to cheerfulness, who is at ease in many situations and is never at a loss for words, might, when he allows such traits to grow beyond their bounds, become a fellow who seeks to gain favour and even wealth through charmingly teasing words that entice and deceive." He spoke, of course, of Wickham, and from the way, Elizabeth's gaze fell, he suspected she knew it. So, he continued. "And a gentleman such as myself, who is adept at seeing flaws in need of addressing, might become cantankerous and rude, and in doing so, cause hurt through disparagement, for he can only see the unpleasant corner of the stage in which he finds himself rather than the entirety of the theatre."

"And a gentleman who is rarely rattled by anything might become indifferent to those things which should stir him to action," Mr. Bennet added.

"Papa," Elizabeth chided in a whispered.

"No, my dear, it is true. And I will add that a lady, whose mind is quick and ready to debate in a moment, might use such talent to create swords that can cut and pierce even her own heart and mind, blinding her to the truth."

Elizabeth's head dipped, and her cheeks grew rosy.

"Ah, my Lizzy," her father said, taking her hand. "Realizing folly is the first step in preventing any further foolishness and in finding wisdom, and..." He winked at her when she finally looked at him, an action that caused Darcy to smile unwittingly. "I declare, I have never had such a pleasant time at a ball. Not once have either of you spoken of lace or feathers. And for that, I am immeasurably grateful."

"Indeed," Darcy muttered.

"Not a favourite topic of discourse for you either, is it?" Mr. Bennet said with a chuckle.

"It most decidedly is not," Darcy replied.

Mr. Bennet chuckled once again. "Then allow me to conclude our discussion as it appears the next set is forming, and I shall not return to my wife with the news that her daughter did not dance at least once at this ball." Again, he winked at Elizabeth, who shook her head and smiled. "There is truth in both positions. One is not right and the other, wrong. In fact, they work best together. Now." He gave her hand one more squeeze before lifting it in Darcy's direction. "I shall leave you youngsters to the dancing and find myself a glass of something refreshing."

He lifted a brow while amusement shone in his eyes. "However, I will not be far away. There shall be no absconding or other such mischiefs. I think we have had our fill for one night."

"I believe you are correct," Darcy assured him before escorting Elizabeth onto the dance floor.

"I must thank you," Elizabeth said as they made their way to where a circle of dancers was forming for a cotillion. "What you have done for my sister is quite lovely."

Darcy drew her to a stop just before they reached their places. "I did not do it only for her."

"You did not?"

Her eyes were wide in astonishment.

"No," he replied with a smile, "my motives were more self-serving than that."

She blinked and looked at him with what he thought might be the most charming expression of confusion he had ever seen. Silently, she allowed him to bring her to their place in the circle. He looked around the group and then back at Elizabeth. He bowed as she curtseyed. They spoke not a word throughout the first half of the dance. Then, in the second half, when they joined hands and circled together, he pitched his tone low and spoke so that hopefully only she would hear. "I wished for my friend and your sister to be happy, this is true. I would do most anything to ensure Bingley is happy, even if it meant my own misery, which I was certain it did."

"I do not understand," she said as they parted once again.

"I will explain, but not here," he replied as they joined hands again. He wanted to pull her from the dance floor, through the side door, and to some secluded alcove so that they might talk in private, but he had promised Mr. Bennet he would not. Therefore, they would have to pass the dance with broken conversation about something trivial such as the weather or, he smiled, books.

"Talking of books while dancing, Mr. Darcy?" She playfully chided him as they left the dance floor.

"Too mundane?" He queried in reply. "Would

you rather canvas the weather or the flower arrangements?"

She giggled. "I did not know you could tease, sir. In fact, I was led to believe that teasing was beneath you."

"Miss Bingley does not know me so well as she thinks she does," he replied. "I enjoy a small amount of teasing. I cannot say that it is a staple in my conversation, but I have had a most excellent teacher. My cousin, Colonel Fitzwilliam, is proficient in the art. I think you and he will enjoy each other's company."

"He seems very pleasant," Elizabeth replied.

"Mr. Bennet, might I have permission to take your daughter for a stroll in the hall?" Darcy asked as they joined her father. "I believe I know of a comfortable chair where you might enjoy a few moments of relaxation and solitude and yet be able to see the length of the hall in both directions."

"I would like nothing better than a few quiet moments in which I could rest my feet." He waved his hand, indicating Darcy should lead on, which Darcy did with gladness.

"You did not ask if I had a partner for this dance," Elizabeth said as they reached the door.

"I beg your pardon," Darcy replied. "Have I caused another gentleman to be left standing?"

"No," Elizabeth admitted, "but that does not mean you should not have asked." Her lips curled upward, and one brow was arched with an impertinent air.

"Forgive me. I was in error."

"I doubt very much that Mr. Darcy cares two figs if another gentleman was left standing instead of dancing with you." Mr. Bennet winked at her gasp before looking this way and that and spying a chair. "That should do quite nicely," he said with a tip of his head in the direction of the chair. "We are spending a week in town," he informed Darcy before he turned to go take a seat. "If I stay longer, my wife will likely fabricate some reason to join us, and then, I shall never see the inside of my book room until a month has passed and my bank account has felt the adventure most severely." He winked once again and left them alone.

"Then, I shall be returning to Netherfield within a week," Darcy said to the back of the man.

"Very good," Mr. Bennet replied without a look backward. "My wife shall be delighted."

"Will you be pleased if I return to Netherfield?" Darcy asked as he and Elizabeth began their stroll.

"Mr. Bingley will accompany you, will he not?"

His brows furrowed slightly at her response. "Yes, but I was inquiring about if you would be pleased if *I* returned to Netherfield. Bingley could return without me. It would not be ideal, but it is not outside of the realm of possibilities."

"Will his sisters be joining him?" Elizabeth asked.

Darcy shook his head. "I am not certain, but it seems Miss Bingley will likely need to remain in town." He stopped walking. "Unless Sir Matthew wishes to join our party. I shall have to discuss that with Bingley."

"Yes."

"I beg your pardon?" He blinked as he was pulled from his contemplation and looked down at her smiling face.

"Yes," she repeated before adding, "I would be pleased if you returned to Netherfield, provided you are not alone and even if Miss Bingley and Mrs. Hurst must join you." She looked down at where her hand lay on his arm. "You said you would explain your meaning about fearing that helping your friend find his happiness would cause your misery."

He nodded. "I did." He drew and expelled a great breath. "I left Hertfordshire because I believed that my heart was leading me away from where duty said I should go, for I found myself enamoured with a lovely, temptingly handsome young lady, who, though she was all that I could wish for in a wife, was not what I thought my family would expect. She did not have great wealth or connections, but, I realized as I spent many an agonizing hour in town, she had my heart."

His lips curled up into a slight smile. He had thought revealing so much of himself and his desires would be more difficult, but to his surprise, he felt at ease — completely and entirely at ease with Elizabeth at his side.

"I thought that remaining in town would cure me of my infatuation, and so I worked to keep my friend in town with me. How could I return to where her spell would be greatest? How could I encourage my friend to pursue her sister when in doing so, I would be binding myself to either a life of misery in seeing her but never having her or the pain of being separated from one who is as close as a brother?"

They had come to the end of the corridor and so stopped and just stood together looking back down toward the other end.

"As time passed, I came to realize that I could not be so selfish as to risk being the cause of my friend's enduring the same longing I was. My sense of honour would not allow it. It was just at this time when I learned of your sister's call at Bingley's home, and I realized then that my belief of her being indifferent toward him, for I truly had not noticed any partiality on her part toward my friend, was grievously in error."

"You did not suspect her regard for Mr. Bingley?" Elizabeth asked in surprise.

Darcy shook his head. "No, I did not, but once I knew the truth, I also knew I could not conceal my error from Bingley. So, I confessed all to him and prepared to be separated from him forever because I could not witness your loving another who was not me."

Her eyes grew wide.

"Bingley is a good friend and would hear nothing of a separation. He refused to let me leave until

I had seen reason. Who is master of me to approve or disapprove of my choice of a wife if I am so fortunate as to ever secure the affections of the one I love? None, save me. My estate is my own, as is my fortune, and I would rather be separated from my relations than from my heart."

"You love me?"

He smiled at her tone of incredulity. "Shocking as it may be, yes. I love you, most ardently."

"But what of..." she clamped her mouth closed as her eyes grew wide.

"My cousin Anne?" he asked. Wickham had likely told her about his supposed betrothal.

Her cheeks grew rosy, and she nodded.

"It is the wish of my aunt that we marry, but we are not betrothed, nor do I have any plans to ever be betrothed to my cousin."

"I should not have listened to him," Elizabeth whispered.

"I have already forgiven you for that," Darcy replied. "I am most happy to set straight what he has twisted in his attempts to disparage me." He turned to look at her fully. "I wish for you to question me so that I might defend myself with the truth. Please, do not feel ashamed and hide any of it from me."

"Are you certain?"

Darcy nodded. "As surely as the sun shines in the day and the moon, at night."

Her lips curved into a relieved smile. "You are so different from what I thought."

"I am different from the man I presented to all of Hertfordshire, and yet, I am also the same. I am not a man without faults. However, I am a man with faults who would beg you to give him a second chance to prove himself worthy of your regard. Please?" He sucked in a breath and held it as she searched his face.

"You love me?"

He nodded as his heart picked up its rhythm and his cravat suddenly became an uncomfortably warm and restrictive piece of clothing.

"I do not know how," she muttered.

"Nor do I, in truth, but I do," he replied.

She shook her head and chuckled. "My mother will never believe it."

"Does that mean you will give me a chance?" His heart felt like it was going to climb its way up his throat and out his mouth if she did not relieve his anxiety soon.

Again, she shook her head and chuckled before turning a beaming face toward him. "Yes, Mr. Darcy, I should like to see if we are indeed companionable." She bit her lip and tilted her head. "Do we call this a courtship or a friendship?"

He knew a ridiculously large grin was spreading across his face. "Both." He lifted her hand from his arm and kissed it. "Thank you," he whispered.

Down the hall, the library door opened, and Sir Matthew, Caroline, and the Hursts exited before Jane and Bingley, who walked arm in arm with their heads close together.

Elizabeth sighed as she saw it and shook her head. "No, Mr. Darcy, thank you, for being willing to suffer loss so my sister could find happiness." She paused and then looked up at him with merriment shining in her eyes. "And for confounding Miss Bingley, so that Jane and your friend could be rid of her."

He chuckled and pulled her a bit closer to him as they made their way to where Bingley and Jane stood with Mr. Bennet.

"Am I to assume from your happy expressions

that I have not one but two daughters who will be delighting their mother by having secured such handsome and wealthy gentlemen?" Mr. Bennet asked.

"I have not yet secured your daughter," Darcy replied. "However, she has given me permission to make an attempt at delighting Mrs. Bennet."

Mr. Bennet chortled. "I wish you success, young man. Now, shall we depart? Or do any of you wish to dance more?"

It was agreed that no one wished to return to the ballroom, and after sending a footman to locate Richard, Darcy exited the Johnson's house, leaving behind family expectations and moving forward with the lady who held both his arm and his heart into what he hoped would be a very happy future.

Before You Go

If you enjoyed this book, be sure to let others know by leaving a review.

~*~*~

Want to know when other books in this series will be available?

You can always know what's new with my books by subscribing to my mailing list.

(There will, of course, be a thank you gift for joining because I think my readers are awesome!)

Book News from Leenie Brown

(http://eepurl.com/bS1el1)

~*~*~

Turn the page to read an excerpt of *Delighting Mrs. Bennet*, book two in the *Marrying Elizabeth Series*.

Delighting Mrs. Bennet Excerpt

Now that Mr. Darcy has secured a courtship with Eliz-
abeth, how will that courtship play out and how will he
finally convince her to accept his offer of marriage? How
it happens won't be at all how Darcy expects it will.

Chapter 1

"How is he?" Darcy stopped pacing the sitting room as his physician, Mr. Westcott, entered.

"I have seen worse." He cast a glance at the others in the room but spoke to Darcy. "Mr. Royston had some difficulty setting the bone. I would not move him for at least two weeks."

"He may stay where he is, of course," Darcy assured Mr. Westcott.

"I suspected you would say that." Mr. Westcott turned his hat in his hand and smiled at Darcy. "I have left instructions for Mr. Bennet's care with

Mr. Abrams, and he informed me that he would find someone to assign to my patient."

He reached down and scratched the head of the black and tan dog standing at his side. "A fine mess you made, lad," he chided.

The dog cocked his head to the side and seemed to smile, utterly unaware of the damage his racing about in a frenzy of fun had caused.

"Stick to chasing rats," Mr. Westcott added with a pat for the happy beast's head.

"I have never had a pup that was so difficult to train," Darcy apologized. He snapped his fingers at the dog and was completely ignored. Every other dog which had come into Darcy's possession had learned to stop and look when they heard his snap, but not Dash.

Dash was his own dog. It was not that he was incapable of learning commands. No, he was an intelligent beast, wily even, and adept at finding all kinds of mischief into which to toss himself with abandon. He was just unwilling to follow a command unless he determined first that it should be followed.

"Strength of character is not so bad a thing." Mr.

Westcott patted Dash's head again. "It is a great asset once it has been properly directed."

Darcy sighed. "That is the struggle." He looked at Dash and made a clucking sound while tapping his leg.

Dash tipped his head so that one ear flopped up as he looked at Darcy and paused for a moment before deciding that standing at Darcy's side would be the thing to do. And he almost made it to Darcy's side before being distracted by a pair of pretty slippers.

"He'll come around," Mr. Westcott assured Darcy. "He's young."

Elizabeth pulled her feet under her chair and, bending forward, scratched Dash's ear while he looked from her hidden slippers to her face and back.

"Our patient is well-settled?" Mr. Westcott asked Mr. Royston as he entered the room.

"He is, sir. He will likely sleep for some time."

"At present, the more sleeping he does, the better," Mr. Westcott said. "I shall return tomorrow, but if anything changes, you know where you can find me."

"Two weeks," Elizabeth said to Dash as Darcy

walked to the door of the sitting room with Mr. Westcott and his assistant. "My father must stay in bed for two weeks, and who knows how long after that it will be before he is walking properly." She leveled a severe look at the animal which was happily accepting her attention. "You were a very naughty pup," she chided.

Dash ducked his head and looked up at her with sad eyes.

"Do not think I will fall for that," Elizabeth said with a chuckle. "You are still a naughty pup."

"Perhaps if you did not scratch his ear while reprimanding him, it might have a greater effect," said Mrs. Gardiner.

Elizabeth sighed. "I cannot help it. His ears just beg to be scratched, and if I do not scratch them, he will attempt to chew my slipper with my foot still in it."

"I should send him to John at Pemberley," Darcy said from the doorway to the drawing room. "John always knows how to get an animal to mind." He shook his head. "Of course, Georgiana would be sorely displeased if I did. However, I do believe he will be confined to Georgiana's sitting room when we have guests take a tour of the house."

He blew out a breath and crossed the room to sit with the ladies. "I must apologize for the damage Dash has caused. There are no words for how dreadful I feel." How did one make amends for his dog tripping a gentleman and causing him to tumble down the stairs, resulting in a broken leg?

"It is not as if you expected it to happen," Mrs. Gardiner said.

"But if he were better trained..." He stopped his protest at the lift of the lady's brow and the incredulous look she gave him.

"Babies, which Dash is, do not always mind their parent. Trust me. I know. I have four children, Mr. Darcy, and there are days I wonder whose offspring they are, for surely my children would not behave in such an inappropriate fashion." She sighed. "But alas, they are mine. However, each possesses his or her own temperament and will. And Dash, I would imagine, is not so very different." She smiled. "I find biscuits work quite well to encourage proper behaviour."

Darcy chuckled. "Dash does enjoy biscuits."

A footman, carrying a leash, came into the room, and immediately, Dash scooted between Elizabeth's chair and the wall.

Darcy took a small piece of cake from the tea tray, which had yet to be removed from the room after the commotion of a falling father and the doctor being summoned. Crouching down, he extended it to Dash. The cake proved to be far too tempting for Dash to ignore, and soon, the footman was leaving the room with Dash trotting happily behind him while Darcy returned to his chair and the room fell silent.

"I should like to look in on my father before we go, even if he is sleeping," Elizabeth said.

"Of course," Darcy agreed. "Is there any way you might be able to stay with him?" Darcy knew it was unlikely, but he also knew that Elizabeth would wish to see to her father's care. From the hopeful look Elizabeth shared with her aunt, he knew he was correct.

"I fear there is not," Mrs. Gardiner answered.

Darcy nodded and again the room fell into silence, save for the ticking of the clock on the table in the corner. In Darcy's mind, it was not right that a man should be without at least someone from his family near him when he was convalescing. The someone should be Elizabeth. She would, no doubt, know best how to cheer her father and keep him entertained. However, without some sort of able-bodied chaperone to ensure that things were kept proper, it was not possible for her to attend to her father without risking damage to her reputation. His brows furrowed as he considered asking his aunt to come for a visit, but the countess was a stranger to Elizabeth, and that would not do. Perhaps...

"What if your mother were to come to town?" Darcy asked.

"My mother?" Elizabeth's eyes were wide.

Darcy nodded. "Yes, your mother. Then you and your sister could stay here, and your father would not be alone."

Elizabeth shook her head, her look clearly telling him that she thought he was not thinking clearly. "My mother will bring all of my sisters."

"I know," Darcy admitted, "but I thought you might wish to care for your father, and I cannot think of any other way to make it possible."

"I would be delighted to care for him," Elizabeth replied, "but my mother?" She turned to her sister. "Jane, tell him he does not want our mother here. In town. At his house."

"It is only two weeks," Darcy argued. "I am certain I could perform the part of host admirably for two weeks." He was almost certain that was true. Surely, two weeks would be endurable.

Elizabeth sent a pleading look to her sister.

"Our mother is trying," Jane said. "Darcy House is so peaceful," she grimaced, "but it would not be after the arrival of our mother." She paused. "And sisters."

Darcy knew Jane was correct, but he was determined to do what he thought was his duty.

"No," he said, shaking his head, "I am inviting your mother and sisters to Darcy House." His stomach twisted at the thought. The more he thought about it, the more he did not know how he would tolerate so much noise in his home, but it had to be done. His dog had caused Mr. Bennet's injury, and Darcy would bear the discomfort of Mrs. Bennet's presence in return.

Acknowledgements

There are many who have had a part in the creation of this story. Some have read and commented on it. Some have proofread for grammatical errors and plot holes. Others have not even read the story and a few, I know, never will. However, their encouragement and belief in my ability, as well as their patience when I became cranky or when supper was late or the groceries ran low, was invaluable.

And so, I would like to say *thank you* to Zoe, Rose, Betty, Kristine, Ben, and Kyle as well as my patrons on Patreon and the readers who faithfully read all those Thursday posts on my blog. I feel blessed by your help, support, and understanding.

I have not listed my dear husband in the above group because, to me, he deserves his own special thank you, for, without his somewhat pushy insistence that I start sharing my writing, none of my writing goals and dreams would have been realized.

Other Leenie B Books

You can find all of Leenie's books at this link
[www.books2read.com/ap/8pOrNn/Leenie-Brown]
or choose to explore the collections below

~*~

Other Pens, Mansfield Park

~*~

Touches of Austen Collection

~*~

Other Pens, Pride and Prejudice

~*~

Dash of Darcy and Companions Collection

~*~

Marrying Elizabeth Series

~*~

Willow Hall Romances

~*~

The Choices Series

~*~

Darcy Family Holidays

~*~

Other Novels ~ Novellas ~ Shorts

About the Author

Leenie Brown has always been a girl with an active imagination, which, while growing up, was both an asset, providing many hours of fun as she played out stories, and a liability, when her older sister and aunt would tell her frightening tales. At one time, they had her convinced Dracula lived in the trunk at the end of the bed she slept in when visiting her grandparents!

Although it has been years since she cowered in her bed in her grandparents' basement, she still has an imagination which occasionally runs away with her, and she feeds it now as she did then — by reading!

Her heroes, when growing up, were authors, and the worlds they painted with words were (and still are) her favourite playgrounds! Now, as an adult, she spends much of her time in the Regency world, playing with the characters from her favourite Jane Austen novels and those of her own creation.

When she is not traipsing down a trail in an attempt to keep up with her imagination, Leenie resides in the beautiful province of Nova Scotia with her two sons and her very own Mr. Brown (a wonderful mix of all the best of Darcy, Bingley, and Edmund with a healthy dose of the teasing Mr. Tilney and just a dash of the scolding Mr. Knightley).

Connect with Leenie

E-mail:
LeenieBrownAuthor@gmail.com
Facebook:
www.facebook.com/LeenieBrownAuthor
Blog:
leeniebrown.com
Patreon:
https://www.patreon.com/LeenieBrown
Subscribe to Leenie's Mailing List:
Book News from Leenie Brown
(http://eepurl.com/bSreI1)
Join Leenie on Austen Authors:
austenauthors.net

Printed in Great Britain
by Amazon

34673205R00131